THE DREAM GUY NEXT DOOR

A GUYS WHO GOT AWAY NOVEL

LAUREN BLAKELY

ABOUT

A sexy, swoony falling-for-the-neighbor standalone romance from #1 New York Times bestselling author Lauren Blakely!

Just my luck - my new next door neighbor is a unicorn.

Yep, the British hottie is clearly a mythical man because - get this - he's a sexy, witty, charming, big-hearted single dad.

Who, wait for it, wants to find Mrs. Right and get hitched.

He's a once-in-a-blue-moon kind of man, and it's a darn shame I'm not on the market. If I were, his accent alone would melt me. Add in the fact that he's a veterinarian, and my animal-loving heart would be flip flopping.

But my heart's on the mend. I'm a single parent like him, and raising my teenage daughter is my top priority. Plus, falling for a guy who shares your property line is a line you shouldn't cross.

Still, I'm an outgoing gal, so I do the neighborly thing and offer to be his dating insider.

Surely, I can help this small town's most eligible bachelor ever navigate his way through all the fantastic single ladies eager to make his acquaintance.

What could possibly go wrong in helping the dream guy next door find his one true love?

So I set him up on one date, two dates, three dates — and I'm about to find out exactly how dangerous my offer is.

THE DREAM GUY NEXT DOOR
BY LAUREN BLAKELY

By Lauren Blakely

To be the first to find out when all of my upcoming books go live click here!

1

___

JANUARY

One fine Saturday that summer

One thing you can count on for certain is the buzz when a new guy moves into the neighborhood.

The other sure bet? That rumor will be rock-concert loud if said newcomer is a stone-cold hottie.

That's the chatter spreading through Duck Falls faster than an image of a sexy celebrity kayaking in the nude trends on Twitter.

The two-story bungalow next to mine on Mallard Lane has been empty all summer—the kind of vacant that crackles and hums with burning questions. Will a family snag it? Will a developer nab it? Will someone flip it and sell it for a mint, driving up the value of all the other homes on the block, including the ones with chipped paint and cracked windowsills?

Or will—pretty please with a serving of looks-like-

Chris-Hemsworth-on-top—a handsome, single sweetie pie move in?

The FOR SALE sign transformed into a SOLD one in June, but the only crumb of intel we Duck Fallsians could scrape together was that an out-of-towner had made the winning bid.

And so the speculation ramped up.

Was the buyer male? And if so, what box did he tick off on forms? Married? Divorced? Widowed? Separated, but still cohabiting, so please keep him far away from me because that's not even remotely close to acceptable?

How about on dating sites? Would ladies deem him to be a smooth-talking player? A cougar chaser? An escape artist? A too-good-to-be-true-er?

No one knew. No one even knew if he was straight.

But by July, the notoriously tight-lipped realtor let slip three glorious words.

Straight.

Single.

Male.

With that settled, emphasis turned to the details. Valeria Rodriquez, owner of the small-batch ice cream shop in the town square, tossed out the first question.

Would he be wildly clever?

The next came from yogini LaTanya Smith.

Might he be deliciously funny?

Polly at the yarn store went so far as to post on the town's online forum: *Anyone know if he likes hedgehogs? I have five now, so I'm looking for a partner who'll pet my hedgehog.*

Yeah, no one knew the answer to that.

Or if that was a euphemism.

Other inquiries have floated through the air.

What if he's a know-it-all? A boring blowhard? A cheating jerkface cad?

Ah, but what if he's kind, smart, sexy, and a god in bed?

A woman can dream—dream of man-i-corns.

And so the ladies do dream here in Duck Falls, population 15,474, and the beloved gateway to wine and olive country. Our hamlet is home to the best combo bookstore-slash-wine shop on the California Coast. The train tracks that run along the edge of town are so Instagram-worthy that you could selfie yourself for days. We love our eponymous ducks and have pink plastic kiddie pools in the town square for them to splash around in. Our sidewalks seem paved with silver, and I don't mean figuratively—we're home to a glitter factory.

All that, and a nose for sniffing out eligible bachelors.

The whole town, it seems, likes to man-watch.

It's the Duck Falls way.

But it's not *my* way.

I'm simply not in the market, nor am I even considering a trip to the man counter. No deli number needed for this woman—no rump roast or ham hock for *moi*. Shacking up, hanging out, and Netflix-and-chilling hold no appeal for me.

But neither does seeming unsociable in this town that's been my home forever. It's a matter of striking the right balance between being politely interested in the town's favorite topic and being *too interested.*

That means there's no escaping when I walk right into a circle of Duck Falls speculation one Saturday morning in early August.

My spawn and I head into the boba tea shop next to the yarn store with no idea what awaits us. A wind chime tinkles as the door swings open, announcing our entrance.

"Good morning, Nina," I say to the chirpy blonde proprietor behind the counter.

"A very good morning to you, January," she says, her face packing a grin that translates into *I'm about to pepper questions in your direction at the speed of sound.* She shifts her gaze to my kiddo. "Hi, Wednesday. Don't let me forget to send you the new content for the blog later today. I wrote a piece on the merits of fruit tea versus black tea."

My daughter smiles. It's her professional grin, and she wears it well—she's the Web developer for half the town's businesses, it seems.

"I will put it on my Google task list to check in with you," she says.

"Google task list," Nina says with utter delight, clasping a hand to her chest. "I love it."

I squeeze my daughter's shoulder—this kid, I swear. She's a badass CEO at age fifteen.

We order, and Nina makes the drinks, sliding me two tall cups locked and loaded, right along with a serving of "So, what's the Mallard Lane dealio?"

Wednesday snags her mango boba, cutting in, "Why

don't you two chat? I'll wait outside. I have a podcast to listen to on new coding techniques."

"New coding techniques," Nina repeats, seeming tickled pink by Wednesday's habits and hobbies. "That's so . . ." She pauses, hunting about perhaps for a trendy word before she says, "*Rad.* It's just rad."

Wednesday smirks. "Super rad," she replies, as if that's something she'd actually say. She knows the value of keeping clients happy.

"I'll be right there," I call out as Wednesday pushes open the door.

Once it's just the women over age fifteen—fine, we're both over thirty-five, but barely, in my case, at thirty-seven—Nina waggles her drawn brows at me, and I know what's coming. She's married, so presumably she isn't scoping the "dealio" for herself. But with a newly single sister, it's no mystery why Nina's fishing for gossip in Mallard Lane waters—for Maya. "Has the guy next door moved in yet?"

And yes, she's angling to catch a big one.

I swipe my credit card over the card reader. "I haven't seen him yet. But I will keep my eyes open."

There. That's just the right level of interest, isn't it?

Nina squees. "You do that. I hear he's moving in today. I'm dying to know if he's perfect for you-know-who," she says in a whisper, even though we're alone.

"Of course. That makes perfect sense."

See? That's a balanced amount of interest befitting a businesswoman who needs to be in good graces with everyone.

I gesture toward the storage room at the back of the

shop. "And you be sure to let me know if you still want me to build you those new cabinets."

Nina's brown eyes go blank for a few seconds, then they flash with awareness before she smacks her forehead. "Oh, I nearly forgot. I'll let you know who I'm going with soon, January. Either you or Big Beams Construction."

Big Beams.

The new franchise of a national carpentry company that loves to underbid the locally owned shops with its 10 percent discount off the competition.

With a smile that says *I hope it's me, but I know it won't be*, I say goodbye, tea in hand, then head outside, shoving aside thoughts of price cuts I can't afford to give.

Wednesday is parked on the green wooden bench in front of the shop, sipping her tea. Her dark-blonde ponytail bounces as she jumps up and pops out her earbuds.

"Learn lots?" I ask.

"I'm pretty much ready to hack into the town electrical grid now if you need me to."

I sigh contentedly. "That's all I've ever wanted. To raise a cybercriminal."

"Well, you got it," she says, bumping her hip against mine as she lifts her cup and takes a drink.

I wag a finger. "No hacking, missy."

She rolls her green eyes, shooting me a droll look, the kind that teenagers are particularly skilled at firing at their mothers. "I don't hack." She pauses, lifts her brows precociously, then adds, "*Yet.*"

"You better not hack *ever*," I say.

We make our way home, passing my friend Alva Chang's hair salon on the corner. This corner is the most silver-speckled in town, thanks to its intersection with the road to the glitter factory. The silver brick road to beauty.

I wave through the window at Alva, who's the spitting image of Ali Wong. She raises one hand, a pair of scissors in it, and brings it to her ear without stabbing herself in the eye. *Call me.*

Later, I mouth, knowing *call me* really means text her.

"Hacking isn't always bad, Mom," says Wednesday.

"How do you figure? It's not like anyone wakes up and says, *Gee, I hope I've been hacked this morning.*"

"Because people don't understand the bennies."

I ruffle her hair, careful not to mess up her deliberately messy pony. "No hacking, K? It's taken me long enough to start a business. I don't need to compete with Big Beams and deal with the scourge that is my own hacker child."

"I'm not *that* kind of hacker."

"Don't be any kind of hacker. Unless you are hacking a recipe for boba tea," I say, savoring another sip then glancing surreptitiously behind me. "Because Nina Clawson makes the *best* boba tea."

Wednesday smacks her lips in agreement. "She definitely does. Also, did you know mango boba is about ten times better than non-mango boba? It's a proven fact."

I arch a skeptical brow. "Proven by whom? By sassy fifteen-year-olds who don't have to suffer through late nights paying bills and therefore don't need the survival boost only caffeine affords?" I lift my oolong tea with the yummy bubble balls to make my caffeinated point, then slurp noisily. A slippery ball slides into my mouth, and I catch it between my teeth then show it off to her. Then I bite into the tapioca and swallow. "Score!"

"I can do that too," she says, then sucks on the straw, trying to capture the ball of bubble deliciousness right as it shoots into her mouth.

She's victorious, showing off her prize before chomping down on it.

I sigh happily and pat her shoulder. "I've taught you so well, Spawn."

"You have, Spawner, but you are also wrong. Coffee is gross, tea is gross, and this is heaven. All beverages are better with fruit. And that's what I hope Nina says in her blog post."

"Ah, to be young and innocent," I declare, taking another life-sustaining sip of my beverage as we wander past the yoga studio where I've tried, I swear I've tried, to Savasana with LaTanya. "But if you continue to insist on this fruit-tea-is-better blasphemy, I'll leave it to you to fend off all the questions about our new neighbor."

She gasps. "You wouldn't dare."

"Try me."

She points at me like I'm a death-eater. "You're not that evil."

"I might be." We slow at the corner of Mallard Lane then turn onto our street.

"I refuse to believe it, even of you."

I tap my plastic cup to hers. "Fine. You're right. I still

like you too much to do that. But remember, that can change at a moment's notice—you've been warned."

"Hmm. I think you're bluffing. You won't stop liking me, because I am literally the best."

Confidence. It's one of the many things I love about this kid, as well as how she makes my budding business look good online. "If you keep sassing me about tea, I make no promises," I tell her. "Feel free to call me the worst mother in the world."

"You're the worst."

We stroll past a yard so lush and green that it looks like a jewel. Betty Juniper is watering the poppies in her garden as she shamelessly peers at the yellow home next to mine. As our steps grow louder, she whips her gaze our way. Excitement shimmers in her eyes, and she calls out in a stage whisper, "Psst! January! I need to talk to you."

Ooh, Betty always has good stuff to share.

"Hi, Betty. How are your flowers?"

"My flowers? Oh, they're fine." She waves her free hand, the garden hose in the other apparently forgotten as it soaks her peonies and poppies and spatters the white picket fence.

"Ahem, Betty." I peer at the ground, which is becoming more of a lake. "You might want to reposition the hose."

"Yes, I think your poppies are donning their life jackets." Wednesday points to the vibrant orange flowers. Betty just blinks at her, so she tries again. "Because they're about to be submerged."

Yeah, this girl has no problem speaking her mind.

Betty's slate-blue eyes bug out as she finally notices the flood, which has broken the banks of the flower bed and is quickly turning into a bog. She fumbles to twist the nozzle so the deluge is more of a trickle. Then she drops the hose, and this woman who is so committed to a green thumb tromps across the lawn, giving absolutely no fucks what her navy-blue wellies do to the wet grass.

She must have something vital on her mind, to put it mildly.

She forges past the fence and marches up to me on the sidewalk. "Listen. About eight minutes and ten seconds ago, I saw a red sedan that looked suspiciously like a rental car drive by."

Oh, that's how we're doing this? We're Miss Marple-ing the single man's every move?

"The car slowed outside the yellow house next to yours, but I couldn't discern whether it pulled into the driveway. But let me tell you, I got a look at the man behind the wheel, and oh me, oh my, he was a kalamata olive."

"Earmuffs," I tell Wednesday.

Cue my daughter's second eye roll of the day. "It's nothing I don't hear all the time, Mom."

"Even so, you don't need to know about the olive scale."

With a third roll of her green irises, my daughter hands me her cup and covers her ears.

Betty's expression is staunchly serious as she dives into a topic worth drowning her perfect grass for. "We are talking full kalamata here. You know what I mean?" She deals me several *girl, we're in this together* nods.

I fasten on a smile, strapping in for the Naughty Betty ride. "You mean you wanted to sink your teeth into him?" I've heard her scale many times, especially over the last month, since every time I've seen her, she asks if I've met the man yet.

"Oh, yes," she says, adopting a deep Barry White bedroom baritone. "Sink them right into his tush."

Hold on a hot second. "How did you see his tush if he was driving?"

She laughs, shaking her head, all very *Silly child, Trix are for kids.* "You don't have to see something to believe in it," she says. "And I believe in your new neighbor's yummy butt." Putting up her hand, she forestalls a reply I wasn't going to make. "But this isn't about me. This is for my youngest daughter, Missy. She's single again, and well, you know how it goes here. Something in the water causes a disproportionate number of women to spring from our wombs."

"That is true," I agree. It's our town's greatest gift and greatest mystery. We are blessed by a fertility goddess, only she seems a helluva lot more fond of girl babies than of boys.

No one quite understands the Athena phenomenon, but we all understand the effects. Duck Falls counts more female-owned businesses than most towns, more women than most towns, and more women in need of a man-bang than most towns.

Might as well call it Fuck Falls.

There you have it—the reason that new men in

town, be they passersby or residents, receive such avid interest.

Or crazed, horny, give-it-to-me-now interest, I suppose.

Betty continues her man-quisition. "Have you seen him yet? Can you verify if it's true?"

"His biteable tush? That would be nice to know, but I haven't seen it."

"So you haven't met your new neighbor? Are you sure? As in absolutely positive?" The skepticism is strong in this one.

"Scout's honor." I hold up two fingers, then I tap my daughter's hands, signaling that she can remove the earmuffs.

"I heard every word," she says dryly, and turns to our neighbor. "Do you want me to text you an update on the olive scale later?"

Betty stares at my kid like she's given her the secret to having a flat belly while eating cake daily. "Yes. Would you do that?" she asks, glomming on to this idea.

I clamp a hand onto Wednesday's shoulder. "She won't be issuing olive-scale reports."

"But maybe consider it," says Betty. "And maybe let me know before you tell the others? I want to line up Missy before anyone else can grab the olive." She mimes squeezing melons with her hands.

"I've always got my eyes open for Missy. She's a hoot, and one of my favorite board game partners."

"And we'll make sure no one else gets the olive but Missy," Wednesday cuts in. I dig my claws into her shoulder, letting her know she's in big trouble now for egging Betty on.

"We—" I begin to express how much that's not going to happen, but Wednesday interjects again.

"Maybe we can discuss it when my mom fixes those spice racks for you?"

Ohhhhhh.

Oh, yes. I see now.

My child is an evil genius.

"They're still not closing properly, right?" Wednesday asks, tilting her head with innocent curiosity as she closes the deal.

Betty seems to like this win-win idea too. Her smile spreads. "They aren't. So frustrating." Turning to me, she asks, "Can you fix my spice rack later? And there's no need for another on-the-house job. I'll pay you."

"Sure. I have some time this afternoon to work on it."

"Great. I'll bake a coffee cake, and we can catch up while you work."

"Sounds like a plan," I say.

"Olives and coffee cake," Wednesday adds.

"Spice racks and coffee cake," I correct.

"Everything and coffee cake," Betty says.

As we leave, my neighbor picks up her hose and resumes drowning the flowers as she scouts down the street.

Once we're a few houses away, Wednesday clears her throat. "You think she considered that the guy in the rental car might be, oh, gee, someone just passing through?"

I laugh in agreement. "That is exactly what I was wondering."

"Also, who needs a man that badly?"

I hold up my hand. "Preach, sister."

She smacks my palm then downs more of her beverage. "I like boys too, but I don't get the *man-session* this town has. Who cares if the neighbor is a hottie or a nottie? There are plenty of other things to do besides date."

"Exactly. I have taught you well."

After more than a decade with a man who didn't love me, I am a happy camper to be single at last.

Single and *not* in need of a date.

Not in want of a man.

Single and truly single.

No men need apply. Not for anything.

I've been teaching my girl the same thing—that you don't need another person to complete you. You are enough.

I believe that with my whole heart.

At the teal mailbox painted with ladybugs—an adorable addition courtesy of my best friend, Alva—we turn onto the stone walkway leading to our porch.

In spite of myself, my eyes swing one house over.

A red sedan is parked in the driveway.

Hmm. Perhaps Betty is Miss Marple after all.

And call me Agatha Christie, because I spy with my little eye a moving truck and a couple of burly men in blue dockers lugging a black leather couch up the steps.

There's no sign of the owner though.

"We'll pop over later and introduce ourselves. See if they need anything," I say as I climb the porch steps.

A door creaks, and a voice rumbles across the yard. "Yes, this is a little quieter than New York City. But I have a hunch it's going to be absolutely fantastic."

I stop in my tracks.

That voice.

He sounds like an English hottie, like Tom Hardy, Daniel Craig, or Henry Cavill.

What are the chances though? That the face will match that kind of a voice?

One thousand to one?

No.

One million to one, easy.

No way can any man have that yummy of a voice and as fine a face to go with it.

He'll be a nottie.

I turn around.

There go the odds.

2

———

LIAM

A few days before

I'm a glass-half-full kind of person.

Life gives you lemons?

Don't just make lemonade. Make lemonade with vanilla bean extract, organic lemons, and homegrown honey from your own beehives and sell it at a roadside stand. You'll make a mint.

Yes, I did that when I was younger. I made a pretty penny with Liam's Roadside Lemonade, thank you very much.

Wake up well before the alarm clock? Log ten extra miles on the bike as the sun rises and the birds chirp, and don't forget to stretch your hammies when you're done.

Sounds like my day yesterday, and I like to think my heart thanks me for the cardio love I give it every morning.

But being asked to diagnose a malady I don't treat? That ranks right up there with eating broccoli.

That happens to me more than one might think. Not the consumption of broccoli—one of the greatest benefits of adulthood is never having to eat a veggie you hate. Goodbye, broccoli. Farewell, brussels sprouts, and see you never, radish.

But I can't escape people telling me about their corns, even though my work has nothing whatsoever to do with feet.

My profession is paws.

Trouble is, when your patients can't speak, their owners make up for it by flapping their gums, mostly about themselves. When someone's beagle has an allergy to fish, you learn about the owner's reactions to salmon, and *Have you ever heard about salmon allergies, and what should I do about it?* When Rover comes in with an upset belly, you're the audience to a soliloquy from his master about his own digestive woes.

To hear or pretend not to hear—that is the question.

But ignoring a client goes against my nature, so I wind up listening to all sorts of ailments every time I examine Fido and Fluffy, Puss and Boots, and Lucy and Rex. I love my job, but this is one of my least favorite parts of it, and that's saying something, because I have to give rectal exams daily.

Thankfully, that's something I *don't* have to do at the last appointment of my last day at my practice on the Upper East Side.

It's simply needle time for Cecily.

I administer a distemper shot to a sleek black cat

decked out in a bejeweled velvet collar, then scratch the kitty's chin. "There you go, Cecily. What a good girl."

The cat lifts her head, eagerly accepting the chin rub —give it up for the cat whisperer in the house—while her owner smiles demurely and taps her lip. "One more thing, Dr. Harris."

"Yes, Blair?"

She flips her red hair off her shoulder and poses her question. "If Cecily is having trouble sleeping, like, say, she's waking up in the middle of the night and can't fall back asleep, what should *I* do?" Perhaps realizing her blunder, Blair straightens, clears her throat, then smooths a hand down the cat's back. "For *her*. What should I do for *Cecily*? The cat?"

Of course. Because so many cats suffer insomnia. It's amazing there's not more research into the problem.

"Well, funny you should ask, Blair," I deadpan. "I see a lot of cats who have trouble sleeping through the night."

"Really?" Blair's green eyes widen, looking delighted by my answer. She must really want validation. Or really not want to see her internist for her sleeplessness woes.

She'll be so disappointed to learn I can't prescribe Ambien.

I nod, still straight-faced. "It's true. It's a very common problem with nocturnal animals."

"I had no idea." She misses my irony completely. "What do you recommend, doctor? Is there something she should take?"

First of all, I recommend asking a human doctor. As in, a doctor for humans.

I don't say that though, because as much as I dislike twofers, they're a part of life as a vet. And being a glass-half-full person, it's not *that* hard to pass along a little tip.

Ugh, I'm such a softie sometimes. If I were a country vet, I'd be that guy with a llama, a goat, and an emu roaming my garden.

Come to think of it, raising an emu isn't such a bad idea. Will I have room for one in Duck Falls, I wonder?

I shake my head, force my straying thoughts back to the present. There will be time later to daydream about patches of land and the possibility of flightless birds.

"For starters, you'd want to look at Cecily's sleep habits," I say, stroking Cecily's chin—such an Upper East Side name for a cat. "Ask yourself: Is Cecily going to bed at a decent hour? Is Cecily drinking too much caffeine late in the evening? Is she turning off her phone?" I rattle off all the bad habits that might lead to poor sleep for, ahem, cats. "And more so, is she looking at her mobile in the middle of the night when she wakes up to use the litter box? That is the single biggest cause of sleep interruptions."

"L-litter box visits?" Blair asks, her brow creasing.

"No. It's the time the cat spends checking out email or Instagram on the phone while in the litter box."

"I had no idea." She sounds as if I've just dazzled her by pulling a rabbit out of a top hat.

"Yes," I say, nodding as I pet the soft, silky Cecily, who purrs with each stroke. "Do you think that might be preventing her from nodding back off? The blue light of screens wakes up the feline brain."

"The blue light of screens," Blair says, like I've handed her the answer to all her problems. Twofer indeed. Though Google would have told her the same thing. Maybe I *should* charge extra for the advice sessions.

"There you go. Maybe you . . . I mean, *Cecily*," I say dryly, finally meeting Blair's eyes and giving her the *I see what you did there* look, "should stop peering at her phone in the middle of the night."

A contrite grimace twists her face, and she dips her head, hand on her chest. "Sorry, it was me. I'm having trouble sleeping, and I do check my Insta at night."

"Yes, I was able to put two and two together. But if the troubles persist, you should see your doctor. One who has an MD. Especially if you're going to need to take something to aid your sleep. But hopefully some good, old-fashioned unplugging will do the trick. I'm sure all those pokes and finger tags will still be there in the morning."

"Finger tags?" Her brow knits.

"Finger taps?" Social media is right up there with broccoli for me.

"Just tags, Dr. Harris. They're just called tags."

"And the tags will still be there in the morning," I revise.

"Of course." She picks up her cat and deposits her in her carrier. "And I'll miss you, Dr. Harris. Good luck with your move."

"Thank you. And I'll miss Cecily. She's a sweet cat." I

show Blair to the door, saying goodbye to my last appointment after more than ten years of taking care of the pampered pets of New York City.

With my hand on the doorknob, a sense of melancholy settles in, but it's mixed with opportunity too.

I'm taking off tomorrow, packing up and heading home. Though leaving hasn't been entirely by choice, I'm determined to make the best of the change.

It's all I can do.

Besides, no matter how annoying it is to relocate, surely moving can't be as bad as eating broccoli.

Or checking a finger tag in the middle of the night.

I shudder.

Nothing is *that* bad.

* * *

But saying goodbye isn't easy either, even for an optimist.

The next morning, I head up the stairs in my Murray Hill apartment building, contemplating the things that make moving hard. It's not the lifting (I hired movers), nor is it the boxing and sorting of stuff (I hate clutter, so there's not much to sort).

It's the *changing* of stuff, and the way packing up clothes, books, and plates makes you think about what you want in life.

What's worth giving in on.

What's worth giving up.

What you truly need for the next year—the next decade, even.

This minute, though, I *need* to do one last check of my apartment before I hand over the keys to the next owner.

I slide mine into the lock and step inside.

An ache slams into my chest as I look around at the empty space.

There's a particular feeling that comes from standing in the skeleton of the home you lived in for a decade.

It's awareness that a part of your life is ending. That you're letting go of something, perhaps a piece of yourself. That awareness burrows deep into my psyche and digs far into my gut too—the sense that not only a chapter but a whole book is ending. I have no idea what the opening scene in the next story will reveal, or if it'll be something I want to read.

But it's not optional.

It's the required text for the next phase of my life.

Parking my hands on my hips, I draw a deep lungful of air, surveying the hardwood floors, the bare white walls, the cupboards. My eyes sweep over the space that now contains . . . nothing.

Nothing at all.

No furniture. No art. No bookshelves.

But I can so clearly see what was here a few days ago before the movers packed up everything.

The black leather couch that's on its way across the country.

It'll look smashing in my new bungalow in Duck Falls.

Or . . . will it?

Hmm. Now that I think about it, maybe I *should* have let go of that couch. It's not best suited to my life these days. The leather and steel that's perfect for a man cave doesn't exactly work with a kid who wants to cuddle up on a comfy sofa and watch cartoons for the gazillionth time.

I picture the glass coffee table that sits on simple chrome legs, now also whooshing its way west.

That will look good too . . . won't it?

Except perhaps glass isn't the best choice either. Seems I have to spray the tabletop clean twelve or three hundred times a day.

I swing my gaze to where the replica Eames chair sat and . . . dammit.

Why did I keep that when it's already acquired so many nicks and scratches?

Maybe it could go in the office of my new practice?

Right. Sure. Great idea. A place crawling with literal animals is no better than a place crawling with one particular species—the dastardly and destructive variety known as a young boy.

Shit.

I should have donated all of my stuff. Maybe I can find a home for it. Who out there wants leather, glass, and steel furniture? Bachelors in need? Playboys furnishing their man pads? Perennially single men in the city?

No one. Absolutely no one.

I groan, cursing myself for holding on to those things. Keeping them three years ago made sense. Keeping them now is the height of foolishness.

But no matter.

Once I'm in California, I'll pop into an IKEA. Replace everything. Be in and out with new stuff in a jiffy.

Except I've only been in an IKEA once. I needed a map and a flashlight to find my way to safety.

I'll gird myself this time. Study the routes, plot in advance. Surely I can navigate a big-box store, even a labyrinthine one.

I take a breath, talking back to my momentary furniture panic.

Everything will be fine.

All I need to do is get through this final look-see, and then I'll be on my way.

Ready to make the best of a tough situation.

I pace across the apartment, making sure nothing was left behind. That's what I came to do this morning—not wonder about the suitability of a stylish sofa or a sleek table.

I step into the bedroom that was home to my king-size bed mere days ago.

That, too, is in transit.

So is my son's twin bed. A bed that I didn't need until a few years ago. But now it's making its way to the other coast, along with the black comforter set, because Thor sheets are no longer cool, dinosaur sheets were decidedly uncool the first time we went shopping for bedding, and apparently all the other colors at Bed Bath & Beyond are unacceptable to the discerning fourth-grader.

I never thought I would know about the sheet preferences of the grade-schooler set. Now I do, as well as whether "dope" or "epic" is the cooler word ("dope" is).

I turn into the bathroom, opening the medicine cabinet and checking the shower one more time. There's nothing left.

I am well and truly ready to go.

I need to go. And I want to go.

Still, it's hard. I try to shake off that clutch of longing, that knot in my chest that wants to tether me here, to this city that's been my home.

I head to the front door and set a hand on the knob for the last time. "Goodbye, bachelor pad," I say. But it hasn't been a bachelor pad for a few years.

Stepping out, I tug the door shut behind me, closing the book on this story.

I bound down the steps, slipping away from my Manhattan life that was once rich with dinners out five nights a week, two-hour visits to the gym, and shows, concerts, wine and cheese tastings, plays and parties, art galleries, and dates, lots of dates.

Out on a sun-drenched Park Avenue, cabs and buses trundle by. My son punches my cousin Oliver's arm, adamantly making a point, it seems. Aunt Jane stands next to them, regarding the two with amusement over the top of her glasses. Quick-witted, gossip-loving, cat-collecting Aunt Jane—she's another part of this city that I'll miss.

"No! Steve Trout is the greatest player of all time," my son insists.

Indignation spreads across Oliver's face, as it well and truly should at the suggestion that a modern-day baseball player could be the greatest of all time—especially someone who plays for the enemy.

"How could you even say such a thing?" Oliver stares at Ethan, bewildered, then at me, thrusting a cup of coffee in my hand. "What have you been teaching him, Liam?"

I shake my head and raise my free hand, denying responsibility for my son's terrible choices when it comes to baseball hero worship. "Trust me, I didn't teach him that sort of blasphemy." I take a vital drink of the coffee, needing the blast of energy it'll bring me. Oliver hands me a bagel next, and I nod my thanks.

My son looks up at me, all big blue puppy-dog eyes and shaggy blond hair. He's hardly like me at all, but the DNA test made it clear that neither hair color nor eye color matter. He's mine, and I'm his. "Dad, you like Steve Trout, don't you?"

I set a hand on his forehead, as if I'm checking his temperature. "Liking a Dodger? Are you feeling okay?"

He huffs. "Steve Trout is the coolest."

Oliver clears his throat. "The coolest," he says, stabbing his finger in the air to make his point, "is Mariano Rivera. A Yankee through and through."

Aunt Jane weighs in, clearing her throat. "The coolest is . . . Reggie Jackson. He was also a Yankee for a spell."

Oliver quirks a brow. "Jane. *You're* not even old enough to have watched him play."

With narrowed eyes, she taps him on the head. As he deserves. "Rephrase, please."

Oliver rearranges his features, barely looking

contrite though. "I mean, how can he be your favorite? He played ages ago, well before you started watching the Yankees."

"I can read. I've read plenty of baseball history books."

I catch Oliver's gaze and mouth, *You're in so much trouble.*

"And all those books say the Yankees are better than the Dodgers," Oliver adds.

Ethan rolls his eyes, laughing. "You're all so weird. It's not like that with me and my friends. We like who we like. Doesn't matter what team they play on. Dodgers, Yankees, Red Sox."

I cover his mouth with my hand and look at Aunt Jane and Oliver. "Forgive him. He knows not what he speaks."

My son licks my hand. Laughing, I peel it off him as he cackles. "Gross," I say. "You're like a dog."

Dancing a victory jig, Ethan says, "Sounds like a compliment. Also, what did you think would happen when you put your hand on my mouth?"

"He makes a valid point," Oliver puts in, clapping my son on the back then pointing at me. "You were kind of asking to get licked, Liam."

"Evidently I must ask for it every day, since I get licked every day. Usually by a cat though," I say offhand.

"And now all the cats of Duck Falls will be giving you a lick," Aunt Jane says, a soft and slightly sad smile curving her lips. She's my mum's sister, and she moved here from England a few years ago. "I'm glad you're going there to help out."

"I'm glad I can help too," I say on a rough swallow, choking back the reasons why I'm helping out. Reasons I fervently wish were different. "But on that note, I should go."

Aunt Jane wraps her arms around me and plants a quick kiss on my cheek. "If you make me linger at a goodbye, my mascara will run, and I will be most upset. Besides, we'll get together for Christmas and other holidays," she says, her voice breaking, something I rarely hear it do.

"Yes, we should be getting on. The airport waits for no one," I say, a note of sadness slipping into my voice that I attempt to shove away before anyone can notice it. At least I hope they won't notice it, this patchwork of family that I have here in New York. They've been my people for the last several years, and it'll be weird not to see them whenever I want.

"I guess this is it, and in all seriousness, I will miss you," I say to my cousin, emotions bubbling to the surface momentarily.

Oliver scratches his jaw and blows out a long stream of air, his tone turning serious too. "Hate to admit it, but I feel the same."

We might give each other a hard time, but we both know the score. We've depended on each other. He's been a regular presence in my life here in New York for the decade I've called this city home. We're two transplants here in the States who have been making our way in Manhattan.

But now I've been called back to the other side of the

country to responsibilities I never expected, but ones I can't turn down.

I haul him and Aunt Jane in for a last hug, then say goodbye to this city.

I'm ready.

I'm sure of that.

As much as you can ever truly be ready to leave a city of millions and return to a small town with a kid you didn't even know you had until three years ago.

Life has a habit of raining lemons, and it's up to you to make lemonade.

* * *

You can't debate the next chapter in your life for too long when you've got a kid on your own. Your job as an only parent morphs by the second. Sometimes you're head cheerleader, sometimes a psychiatrist, and sometimes a chief janitor.

After Ethan and I settle into the second row of the plane, the flight attendant hands him an orange juice. "Thank you," he says with a gap-toothed grin. He lifts the cup to his lips, but it wobbles, and he spills the drink on the armrest, the seat, and the floor.

"Sorry, sorry, sorry." The apology flies out of him at Mach speed.

"No worries. We'll clean it up," I say. This is a piece of cake compared to what I clean up daily—no, hourly —at work.

But before I can track down a napkin, the superhero

known as a first-class flight attendant, who has radar to rival an FAA antenna, swoops back over with a cloth and wipes down the seat, then the armrest, and the floor.

"All better," she says with a lip-glossed smile and a cheery grin.

My son smiles back. "Thank you so much."

She gives a little curtsy. "You're quite a gentleman, and your accent is adorable." She makes a little bopping gesture at his freckled nose.

"Thanks," he says as he flops back into his seat. "I'm American, but my mom was British and my Dad is too." He pats my shoulder as if the flight attendant might be confused about who his father is.

She shoots a bemused look at both of us. "That would definitely give you an accent."

Ethan pokes my arm, then slides into a right proper imitation of me, waggling a chiding finger. "*Now, don't forget to do your science homework, young man. Science is quite possibly the most important subject.*"

"Well, it is," I say, standing my ground.

"I couldn't agree more. Your father is right," the attendant says, leaning in a little closer, her eyes on Ethan the whole time, and I like that she talks to him directly. That's how it should be. "Now, promise me something, little man."

"Sure," he says, sitting up straighter, eager for her command.

She does that air bop again. "That you'll let me know if you need anything. Anything at all." Her voice drops. "Like ice cream. Or brownies. Or a special movie."

"Ice cream. Brownies. And a special movie, please."

Gently, she pats his head. "I'll make it happen."

She stops at the row behind us, and I turn to Ethan, chief cheerleader kicking in as we click in our seat belts. "Okay, so this is it. Soon, we'll get warm nuts. And do you know what that means?"

He giggles. "You said 'warm nuts.'"

"Yes, I did. And they're delicious," I say, keeping a straight face. "Also, they're a symbol. A demarcation between one thing and another."

"Dad. *Nuts.*" He can't stop laughing.

"Yes, nuts. A tasty snack," I say, keeping a deadpan expression.

A cackle bursts from him, clearly located in the seismic epicenter of his funny bone. He grabs my arm. "You can't say that."

"I can, and I did. And do you want to know why I like warm nuts?"

More chuckles emanate from Ethan, but he tries to collect himself. "Why?"

"Because it means we're off. We're making our ascent, heading to our next adventure."

His expression turns worried. "What if I miss New York? And Florida too?"

The subtext isn't lost on me. New York is all he's known for the last few years. Florida was all he knew before then.

But laughing is something he's done in both places. Or so I was told.

"We can always visit," I say, giving him my best *we've got this* smile, even though there's no need to visit Florida now. Nothing familiar for him there.

"We should visit New York, then," Ethan says with a nod, resolute.

And I couldn't agree more. We'll still have people in New York who we'll miss. "We will absolutely come back and visit."

"California is fun though. I've liked it every time we've visited Nan and Pop. But do you really think it'll be an adventure?"

I stroke my chin, pretending to consider this deeply, but speaking from the heart. "Let's see. We're moving to the town where I spent my last two years of high school. We're going to see Nan and Grandad a lot."

"Now that I'll be seeing him regularly, can I call him Pop instead? It's easier. I like Pop better."

"I'm sure he'll be just fine with that," I say, picturing my dad, his sturdy demeanor, his tough-as-nails approach, and his fierce love of his grandkids. He won't care at all—plus he has other matters on his mind. "And my sister and her kids will be there. And we have a pool. Hello, a pool! With a waterslide." He'll love the pool. Of that I'm sure. Our building in New York had a gym and an indoor pool that was practically Ethan's second home. He's always loved the water.

"I might be a fish," he says.

"Please. You're a dolphin."

"You're right. Dolphins are cooler too."

"You can go full dolphin in California. So yeah, let's make a promise that we won't let it be anything but a great adventure."

A smile spreads immediately on his face. He offers a fist for knocking.

When you're a fourth-grader, handshakes have been passé for ages.

"Then I'm up for adventure," he says.

A few minutes later, as the plane taxis on the tarmac, the helpful attendant swings by once more, stopping at our seats. "I forgot to ask. What takes you gentlemen to California today?"

Ethan points at me. "My dad is making me move."

"Ah, so someone doesn't want to?"

"At first I didn't. But he said it'll be an adventure. So maybe it won't be so bad."

"Moving is definitely an adventure. I was born in California, then I moved to Louisiana, and then to Missouri, and then to Alaska, and then to Arizona. And they were all adventures."

"Did you like moving so much?"

She seems to mull it over. "It can be hard to leave your friends. But you know what I love about moving?"

He sits up straighter in his chair. "What?"

"New experiences, new people, and new chances."

"I like meeting new people," he says.

"Then I bet you'll love it."

The attendant takes her seat by the door while Ethan settles in with his AirPods and a game on his phone, swiping across the screen in hot pursuit of candy, or boxes, or gems, or other absurd things.

I pop on an audiobook on the science of sleep.

Soon, we're soaring into the sky.

As the jet reaches higher, I repeat in my head, *New experiences, new people, new chances.*

Even though this move is about my family, those words still resonate with me.

That's where the true awareness comes in.

An awareness of what I'm choosing to step into, and what I'm choosing to leave behind.

After years of being devoutly single, and then a few more of being a devoutly single dad, I've decided to embrace a particular aspect of this move—a brand-new chance.

I'm ready to date again.

Dare I say, I'm ready to find the one. To settle down.

Call me a unicorn.

I'm the guy who's looking to get hitched.

Maybe I'll find her on the other side of the country.

3

———

JANUARY

That fine Saturday in August when the hottie moved next door

I can frame a door, work a power saw, and build a cabinet. Call if you need someone to fix a sink, repair a pipe, and change a tire.

I'm wired for the practical.

I'm *not* a swooner.

My brain doesn't go upside down when I see a handsome man. I don't faint over muscled arms or chiseled jaws, and I don't melt over buttery British voices and *GQ* faces.

I did the whole swoon-over-a-pretty-boy routine with my ex, and that was a mistake akin to installing a toilet without connecting the pipes (awesome child notwithstanding).

I learned my lesson, so I refuse to flutter my lashes or hump a hottie's leg.

Especially when he's my new neighbor.

But giving him a welcome gift?

I should have thought of that sooner.

It would be terribly rude if I didn't pop over right the hell now with a welcome-to-the-neighborhood basket of goodies.

After I close the front door behind me, I set my boba tea on the bright orange coffee table—a flea-market find that I painted with Alva. I take a deep, fueling breath, snapping my fingers, trying to think.

I need to give him a gift. What do we have handy?

Think, think, think.

Wine?

That's always safe . . . unless someone is an alcoholic.

Some of the honeysuckle soap I made last week?

That could work, but will he suspect I'm secretly saying, *You smell?*

Maybe something from my garden? Cilantro? Arugula? Tomatoes?

Who doesn't love tomatoes?

"How about you offer to hammer anything he needs nailed? That could be your welcome gift," Wednesday says as she heads to the kitchen and drops her plastic cup in the recycling bin. Grabbing mine, I follow suit. "Or there's a half-full bottle of fancy mustard in the fridge," Wednesday adds. "Offer him that."

"I'm going to pretend you didn't just say that." I grab a pretty wicker basket from the counter, remove the loaf of bread in it, then grab some scissors.

"Are you going to frolic over there with your basket like the Easter Bunny?"

"No, Spawn. I'm going to give him some cilantro and daisies."

"Nothing says 'Welcome to the neighborhood' like the most-hated garnish and the nastiest-smelling flowers," she says.

I shoot her a sharp look. "Wrong. Everyone knows sunflowers are the stinkiest flowers."

"Oh! You're right. Those are gross."

I scurry across the kitchen to the back door.

"Why are you acting like you're about to run a race?" she calls out.

I snap my gaze back to her as I dart onto the door-mat. "Because," I say, flapping my free hand, "we have a new neighbor, and we have to give him something."

She follows behind as I rush to the garden in our yard. "So you're giving him . . . vegetables?"

I shoot her a look. "Everyone loves fresh veggies." I kneel beside my garden beds, snipping some cilantro, setting it gently in the basket, then adding some radishes. Radishes are making a comeback. I've seen them all over the menus at both fancy hipster restaurants and cheap hole-in-the-wall joints.

"No," she says. "Everyone loves peaches. Everyone loves cookies. Not everyone loves veggies."

I flap my arms around, gesturing to the yard. "Well, I don't have cookies or peaches."

"Maybe get some, then?"

"I'll start with veggies. He can make a salad."

"Awesome. Radish salad sounds delish. Let me know if I can have some too."

"You're now banned from salads for your impudence," I say, and snip some daisies too.

She pumps a fist. "I'm going to make sure you hold to that promise. Also, Dad didn't love veggies," Wednesday points out.

I point at her. "No, he was allergic to them. Big difference. Tomatoes gave him hives."

"Cilantro gives me nightmares."

Laughing, I shake my head. "If that's the worst of your nightmares, consider yourself lucky."

"If I never eat cilantro again, I'll consider myself very lucky," she retorts as I pluck some radishes.

"You don't eat cilantro at all. You refuse anything that includes it. And with panache too." I launch into an imitation. *"Thanks, but I'm going to decline the cilantro-lime rice.* Also, I believe radishes are the new black."

Wednesday shakes her head. "No. Candy is the new black. Boba is the new black. Black is the new black. Radishes are the new brown."

I set the flowers in the basket alongside the veggies, then I stand and tilt my head. "The new brown?"

"As in, no one's favorite color."

"Mark my words. He'll love the radishes." I leap up the steps, Wednesday on my tail.

"I'm going with you just to laugh when he crinkles his nose at them."

I roll my eyes, stop at the sink, wash the radishes, dry them, then line the basket with a blue checkered cloth. After setting the radishes and the cilantro in next, I snip the stems of the daisies, find a piece of string, and tie it around the flowers. Then I reach for a bar of honeysuckle soap and add it to the mix.

"Voilà."

"Don't say I didn't warn you."

I leave the gift on the counter for a moment. "Be right back."

Hurrying down the hall, I hightail it through my bedroom and pop into the bathroom, where I check my reflection and smooth my brown hair.

I am not in the market for a man. No way, no how, not at all.

But one should look one's best when meeting the new neighbor.

That's just common courtesy.

I tuck a strand of loose brown hair behind my right ear, touch up my lip gloss, dust on some powder, and finally peer left, then right. I run a hand along my neck.

I'm thirty-seven, so my neck is still . . . mostly smooth. My forehead though? I could go for Botox if I wasn't terrified of needles. I rely on self-administered *Bangtox* instead, so I finger-comb my hair over my forehead.

"Ready," I say softly to my reflection. A tingle dares to rush down my chest, heating me up, and I blanch.

What was that?

I set a hand on my chest.

I barely got a good look at him. I cannot be having a reaction to my neighbor already.

I'm not, I'm not, I'm not.

I ignore that tingle. No, I do better than ignore it. I tell it to go the hell away and never come back.

There. That'll teach my body to have reactions to sexy neighbors with swoony voices that I do not, cannot, will not swoon over.

I turn on my heel and leave.

But not before I duck into my closet, yank my T-shirt over my head, and pull on a pink V-neck.

Well, pink is my favorite color.

I head to the kitchen to grab the basket. "Shall we?"

Wednesday peers up from the couch, eyeing me over her phone. "I'm a pawn in your scheme."

"And how's that?"

"You're just using me to make it look like you're not totally checking him out."

A blush crawls up my cheeks. "I'm *not* checking him out."

She wiggles a brow. "Tell that to the jury."

"Also, you offered to come along," I say, as I hoist the basket on my hip and grab a hammer from the orange table. Just in case Wednesday was right.

We head out the front door, and I let the screen door fall behind us with a resounding click.

I don't need to tell anything to a jury, because the judge of me knows the truth, the whole truth, and nothing but the truth.

I'm not totally checking him out.

I'm *slightly* checking him out.

And I cannot wait to tell my friend Alva all about the sexy man next door.

4

———

LIAM

All things being equal, Ethan is pretty content here.

First goal accomplished.

Wait.

"Content" is the wrong word.

"Jazzed" might be better, since he's conducting a full inspection of the pool.

"I need to go swimming *noooooooooooow,*" he announces, bending over the edge and dipping a hand in the water. I desperately hope this—the fun he'll have swimming with me, and soon with his cousins when they come over—will help him love his life here and not miss what he had in Florida. It's a life I know little about, but one I imagine was full of endless hours in the water.

"How about later instead of now? We should go talk to the movers, make sure they know where to put everything."

"Fine, but later I want to swim. *Please.*"

"And you will, Dolphin," I say.

He makes a Flipper sound as I usher him back into the house. We stayed at my parents' place last night so we could arrive here rested and ready to meet the movers. I stop to chat with them now, and they tell me it'll be about twenty minutes to assemble the beds they brought in, so they'll be busy for a while.

I thank them, stopping to grab a picture frame from a box—simple, shiny metal, but I'd recognize it anywhere. I set it on the coffee table. A pang of longing punches at my chest as I look at the shot of Ethan with his arms wrapped around his brown-and-white cattle dog from years ago.

What was that day like? How often did he hug that dog? Swim with her in the ocean?

Things I'll never know. A chance I never had.

I tap the photo out of habit, maybe for luck, maybe as a reset to clear away the longing I feel when I look at it.

We head out the front door so I can make sure I've grabbed everything from the rental car.

I stop short when I glance next door.

The realtor mentioned there's a kid living there. Seems there's a kid and a mom—a logical deduction, since most minors do require parental care.

And this mom looks positively hot as . . .

Wait. Settle down.

I shouldn't look at my neighbor like that.

I should not stare at her trim figure. Her short jean shorts. Her pink T-shirt. Her waves of chestnut hair.

I focus on the kid.

I gesture to the girl heading down the steps. "See? There are even kids next door. This is perfect."

My son tilts his head and sends a *what are you talking about* look my way. "Dad, she's twenty. She's not a kid."

I arch a brow. "Twenty? I'm pretty sure she's not twenty. I bet she's eleven," I say, peering at the young lady. I mean, eleven is possible, right?

I wave, and they both wave back, and I do not stare at the mom. I do not watch as she walks down the stone path in their front lawn, a sway to her hips, a soft smile on her face. I do not gaze at her every step.

"On what planet is she eleven?" Ethan asks as they come closer.

"The planet of eleven-year-olds?" I toss back. Fine, maybe he's right that she's not eleven.

But she's not twenty.

"Look, all I'm saying . . ."

As the pair turns toward my house, I swat his arm, stand up straighter. "They're coming over. Act normal."

"You act normal," he hisses.

"I'm always normal."

"You're so not normal at all," he counters.

This kid. I swear, I don't know where his cheek comes from.

As I wait on the porch, I do my best not to drink in the sight in front of me.

Because my new next-door neighbor is a fox.

And sexy neighbors are incredibly off-limits.

Sexy neighbors are at the top of the list of forbidden fruit, right along with employees, friends of your sister, and ex-girlfriends of your mates. I've never set foot in any of those dangerous territories, and I don't intend to start now.

"Hi there," she calls as she heads up the path, and I walk down the steps to meet her.

Them.

Both of them.

"Hello there. Nice to meet you, neighbor." I pat myself on the back for sounding thoroughly amiable and not at all like a guy in a bar chatting up a luscious lady.

Her smile is radiant, highlighting the constellation of freckles that covers her nose and her light-blue eyes that sparkle.

Damn, she's quite pretty close-up too.

I extend a hand, and we shake. "Hi, I'm Liam. I just bought this house. Which I suppose is obvious because I am moving into it. Because that's what you do with homes you've just bought. You move into them."

Okay. Yeah, that's blatantly obvious too.

I swear I've spoken to women before. I've spent most of my twenties and plenty of my thirties speaking to women. I don't know why it's suddenly weird to speak to *this* woman.

Maybe it has something to do with the tattoos running down her arms. Or the work boots on her feet. Or the hammer in her front pocket. Of course, a hammer shouldn't make it difficult to speak to a woman, but it does make me curious. "In any case, it's nice to meet you."

She smiles, a grin that should be gracing toothpaste tubes. "It's a pleasure to meet you too. I'm January. This is my daughter, Wednesday. She's fifteen, going on twenty."

Ethan shoots me an *I told you so* look as I shake Wednesday's hand then introduce my nearly ten-year-old.

Ethan shakes hands with both women, then says to Wednesday, all tough, "I don't need a babysitter."

"I wasn't going to offer to babysit," she says. "I have a job."

"Cool. Just letting you know," he says, acting so nonchalant. "What's your job?"

"I'm a hacker. I hack into my neighbors' accounts."

January's jaw drops. "Wednesday."

Her daughter grins wickedly. "Sorry. Just kidding."

January sets a hand on Wednesday's shoulder. "She's a little sassy. A little sarcastic."

"Fortunately, we're fluent in sarcasm," I say.

January wipes her free hand across her forehead. "Whew. We are so not hackers. But we are vegetarians, so I brought you a few things from our garden."

Peering into the basket, I catch sight of radishes, and I flinch.

Ethan smacks my arm, chuckling.

January's brow knits, and her daughter laughs. "I told you," Wednesday whispers. "The new brown."

Ethan points at me. "He hates veggies." He peers into the basket. "He hates radishes the most."

And the lovely brunette winces. "Shoot. Really?"

That's a cringe. That's most definitely a cringe.

"He really, really hates them," Ethan says, digging me deeper into the hole.

Wednesday raises a hand. "I told her. No one wants veggies as a gift. Especially radishes or cilantro."

"Do you hate cilantro too?" January asks, the cringe factor still high.

"It's not that I hate cilantro, per se," I say, trying for diplomacy.

"He thinks it tastes like soap. And it does," Ethan says.

"I like soap," I put in, as if that makes things better.

"Soap is good," January says.

Wednesday smiles and offers Ethan a hand for high-fiving. "But who wants to eat soap?"

"Not me," he says, then points to the back of the house. "I have a pool. Want to see it?"

"Sure."

In seconds, they disappear, heeding the siren call of chlorinated water as I stand on the porch with a basket of veggies I won't eat and my sexy new neighbor with her work boots, tattoos, and that smile I want to kiss off.

But I won't.

Because she is off-limits. Kissing the smile off of one's neighbor's face isn't neighborly behavior at all.

"Sorry about the radishes," she says. "I guess they are the new brown, rather than the new black."

"I completely appreciate the gesture though," I say warmly, so she'll know that flinching at the first sight of radishes isn't what defines me as a person.

"There are flowers in there too," she offers. "And a bar of homemade soap."

"Because I smell?" I deadpan.

She chuckles. "I was worried you'd say that."

"Oh, I can take a hint. But as I mentioned, I do like soap." I peer into the basket, a smile tugging at my lips as I spot the daisies. "Ah, my favorite flowers. My mum likes these."

"And the flowers remind you of your mom. I'm batting zero today," she says, a little forlorn.

I furrow my brow. "I like my mum. So it's a compliment."

"Oh."

"Does that surprise you?"

"No? Yes? I don't know."

I laugh. "Sorry. The gifts are lovely."

She laughs and gives an easy shrug. "Most men don't admit to liking their moms. Also, you can feed the radishes and cilantro to the local raccoons if you'd like."

"Actually, raccoons are also not the best market for offerings of cilantro."

"They're not?"

"No. They like nuts, seeds, fruits, eggs, insects, frogs, and crayfish," I answer seriously.

She deals me an inquisitive stare. "Are you a raccoon-ologist?"

"Sort of," I say. "I'm a vet."

"I'm a carpenter."

My eyebrows rise as I point to her pocket. "That would explain the hammer in your pocket."

"Oh, no. The hammer is for when I lock you up in my basement."

I play along. "I was hoping you'd be game for that. Want to go now?"

She laughs. "Actually, my daughter told me the best

housewarming gift would be to offer to hang pictures or art for you. And, as is the case with most things in life, she was right."

"Hold on. You're saying I get soap, flowers for Mum, and your picture-hanging expertise?"

"You left out the radishes and cilantro."

"No. I just didn't get to them yet. They're for the raccoons. I'll leave them out tonight for the bandits."

"Then I want a report tomorrow," she says.

For a second, I simply stand there, enjoying, much more than I should, the unexpected, delightful view of my gorgeous neighbor.

My off-limits neighbor.

Must not consider her an option for the dating plan.

I glance around, trying to think of something else to do than stare at her lovely face. "Want to see the inside?"

"I would love to."

I show her into the house as two guys leave the bedroom and pull a mirror from a box.

"Any idea where you want this, sir?" one of the guys asks.

I glance around, not quite sure. "You can just leave it against the wall."

January lifts her chin, nodding at the guy. "Hey, Joshua. How's Maggie? She just turned one, right?"

"She's walking now," the guy says with a pleased-as-punch grin.

"Excellent. I bet she's a handful."

"And we love it." Then he addresses me, pointing to the front door. "We're going to grab some more things. Almost done. You don't have much."

"I'm a minimalist," I say.

"Cool," the guy says, and strides out.

I turn to see January has a hand on the leather couch, and she's nodding knowingly. "I notice you've got a whole man-pad vibe going on here."

"You think so?" I ask, as if the thought never occurred to me.

"I mean, it's hard to tell with all the black, white, and chrome. But if I *had* to guess . . ."

"Hmm. What do you know? Seems I do." Then I shrug. "Honestly, I think it might be time to ditch it."

"You don't like the look?"

"It seems . . . impractical," I say, gesturing to the yard to indicate the kid. "I was thinking when we left New York that maybe it was time to torch all the furniture."

"Go furniture-free? Sleep on the floor?"

I laugh. "No. I meant finally get something that doesn't scream *I'm single.*"

An eyebrow lifts. "Are you *not* single?"

"I am definitely single. Very much so. But I don't think I need the whole black-and-white-and-chrome look anymore."

She peers around my monochromatic home. "Yeah, there is definitely a bachelor aesthetic working here."

"Tell me about it. Even my son has black bedding. We don't own anything that isn't black or white."

"What about gray? Do you have anything gray?"

I screw up the corner of my lips, considering. "We might have a few gray items. But gray is just a variation. New Yorkers aren't actually allowed to own furniture that's not black-and-white."

"Oooh," she says with an exaggerated nod. "I've heard, too, that single men are limited to items made only of chrome, steel, or titanium."

"Don't forget iron. That's a very manly substance, and we like to have lots of iron tables, spikes, and stakes."

"So manly." She glances again at my black furniture. At my glass table. At the entirely colorless scheme that doesn't fit in this bright yellow bungalow. "Are you truly thinking of going furniture shopping?"

"Yes, but I fear I might never emerge from IKEA. I've heard tell of a secret fast track to the exits, known only to the most experienced shoppers. The rest of us have to follow the winding trail like sheep, and somehow I always get caught behind a slow-moving family with all day to shop when all I want is a desk lamp."

She stands and brushes her hands over the front of her shorts. "Why don't I give you a better house-warming gift? I can take you shopping, Liam."

"For furniture? You'd do that?"

She smiles. "You're my neighbor. Of course. It just so happens that I know the secret route through IKEA. Also, it only seems fair—because I hate your furniture as much as you hate radishes."

"Is it possible to hate something *that* much?" I counter, enjoying her sarcasm.

She pats the couch. "Yup. I detest it."

"Well, my furniture is the new brown."

"Then I'll be your furniture Sherpa. Are you free tomorrow?"

"As a bird," I reply, and she laughs.

"Ah, a vet who makes bird jokes. I'm sure that wins you many clients."

I laugh too, a bit surprised at how well this move is going so far.

That is, if living next door to a pretty, sarcastic, helpful woman I'd love to ask on a date but can't is a good thing.

But I can make the best of it.

I'll be friends with the world's sexiest neighbor with a tool belt and short shorts.

That ought to be easy.

Said. No one. Ever.

5
___

LIAM

As I turn the rental car onto a curving road in neighboring Lucky Falls, Ethan tosses out yet another option for a permanent set of wheels.

"Hovercraft? That slaps. Have you considered it?"

"I have not. Tell me why it *slaps*," I say, filing that new slang away in my drawer of Things Kids Say These Days. "Because I'm totally open to a *dope* hovercraft, but I need to know exactly why that should be at the top top of my list. Why should it be above, say, a Subaru?"

He rolls his eyes and huffs, possibly puffs, with the disdain of youth. "Please tell me you're not getting a Subaru, Dad."

I maintain a straight face as I drive. "Why should I not get a Subaru? Isn't that what dads do? I could also get white trainers and a braided leather belt."

He recoils in the seat, a full-body shudder I catch in my peripheral vision. "No. Just no. That is . . . You can't come home if you do that. Also, just call them sneakers."

"Yo. Sneakers. How's that?"

"Sort of better."

I laugh. "So, tell me more about the hovercraft and why it's better than a Subaru."

He taps his fingers on the dashboard, full of energy. "Because they're cool. Reason enough."

Flipping the turn signal, I slow at the corner. "Cool is, indeed, reason enough."

"Then can we get a Bugatti?"

"Sure. Want to buy it today?"

"Yes!"

As we slow at a fork in the road, I wiggle the fingers of my right hand. "Crack open the piggy bank, then, and fork over some coin. Do you know what they cost?"

He arches an *I have no clue* brow. "A few thousand?"

I point high up. "A little higher."

"A hundred grand?"

My hand stretches toward the ceiling of the car.

"A million?"

"Something like that."

He glances out the window for a moment, then back at me. "Then how about a Batmobile? Maybe we should just get one of those."

"Why didn't I think of that?"

As we near my parents' house, his expression turns serious for a second, earnest. "I have something to tell you."

"What do you have to tell me?" I ask, keeping it light but feeling cautious, in case this is the moment when he confesses that he hates this move.

"It's weird seeing you drive."

Laughing, I answer him, "It's weird to drive. I didn't

drive for years in New York."

"I never once saw you drive in the city. Wait, did you drive that time we went to Saint Lucia?"

"No, that was your butler. Of course that was me. Who else do you think drove us?"

He shrugs helplessly. "I don't remember."

"Well, it was me," I say as I turn into my parents' driveway. "Your father."

"You drive really slow."

"It's safer. Also, driving is like eating radishes."

"You hate it?"

"So incredibly much. It's the worst."

"You should just get a bike, then. Well, another bike. You can't use your racing bike," he says.

True. My racing bike is for just that, though I don't race to place in the centuries I train for. I race for exercise, to hit goals, and for the accomplishment—to crest five mountain passes, traversing one hundred miles in a mere eight hours.

Or something like that.

"So just a regular bike?" I ask. "A tooling-around-town bike?"

"Yeah, you should do that. Since you like to ride, and so do I."

That's not a bad idea. A bike sounds kind of perfect. I cut the engine and look at him. "Should we go bike shopping together later?"

He shrugs happily. "Works for me."

It's almost too easy, the way this move is working for him.

But I want to make sure he's okay with all the

changes. "Hey," I say, setting a hand on his arm.

"Yeah?"

"You doing okay with everything? With being here? With missing New York?"

He nods, but there's still a hint of sadness in the curve of his mouth. "Sometimes I miss Florida too."

"Do you remember much about it?" I ask, bracing myself for whatever he might tell me. There was a long span of time when he missed his old life terribly.

"No. But I remember I liked it there." He waves toward my parents' house. "But I like it here too. Because of Nan and Pop, and everything else, and the baseball camp I'm going to, and the pool. And Spencer," he says, naming one of his cousins.

"Good." I punch him lightly on the arm.

"And because we can adopt a dog now, right?"

Ah, there it is. He's wanted a dog for as long as he's been in my life, but my place in New York was pet-free.

"Do you miss Katrina?" I ask. That's the dog his mom had when he was younger. She told me as much when she showed up.

He likes books, baseball, and dogs. He'll eat nearly anything, but he does love sweets. Don't give him too many. He falls asleep instantly at night, so make time to read during the day. Use a night-light, since that's what he's accustomed to. Also, he still misses Katrina, an Australian cattle dog mix I had who went to the Rainbow Bridge last year. And he likes to talk, and to laugh. That's about it.

Oh, one more thing. He might be a fish. You'll never get him out of the water once you let him in.

That's what she told me—the care and feeding of the

son I never knew I had.

I've been ready for the dog request ever since I told him we'd be living in a house and not a flat.

"I don't remember Katrina," Ethan says. "But that picture of her and me makes me think I liked her a lot. So, I want another."

"It will be after school starts, but the answer is yes." Fact is, I'd like one too. Because . . . dogs.

Also because . . . it's about fucking time.

I won't have to wonder what the days were like when he hugged a dog, threw a ball to a dog, or played with a dog. I'll see them all, experience them all.

Something I didn't have before.

Something I want desperately.

"Yes!" He pumps a fist. "I love it here, then."

Perhaps that's the joy of being his age. You're not too entrenched in your life. You're still open to change. You're malleable and flexible. And you're still wildly confident, enough to walk up to peers, determined to be friends.

It's harder when you're a little older. As I stare at my parents' red home with white shutters and window planters, a crest of nostalgia clobbers me like a rogue wave in the ocean, slamming into me out of the blue. It sweeps me back in time to when I was an angsty and emo sixteen-year-old forced to relocate from England to the States because my father had landed a chance to teach at a veterinary school here and practice in the States as well. Such an opportunity for him, but hell for me.

I'd lived in the same small town in Surrey my entire

life, and the last thing I'd wanted was to move six thousand miles away to a small town in California. I'd hated being uprooted, so I'd handled it by tucking into my room, slamming the door, and blasting bands like The Cure and The Smiths. I'd worn black and cultivated an air of *fuck off, world.* I went on like that for months—head down, teeth gnashing, thoroughly pissed off.

Until an outgoing girl with frizzy brown hair and big green glasses noticed my scores on science tests and invited me to join the Science Club. The club members figured out I was uncannily good at all things chemical and biological, plus numbers and data as well, and they recruited me. For experiments. For projects. For general geeking out.

At last, I had found my people.

Fellow animal lovers, science geeks, and book nerds.

Some of them are still here in Lucky Falls, one town over from Duck Falls, but some have scattered to San Francisco. Others are farther afield across the United States. Some of them I'll no doubt see in the coming weeks and months. Others I may never see again.

But even so, meeting them, realizing my strengths, started me down the path I'm on today—the glass-half-full one, the optimistic one, the found-what-I-want-to-do-in-life path.

The one where I followed in my father's footsteps.

That's what I'm doing now, only it's a little bit harder this time because *everything* is harder for him, and it's becoming more so by the day. He can no longer run his practice, and he's kept that fact under wraps. That's why the realtor kept my name confidential. If it got out that I was the one who had nabbed the house—Liam Harris, DVM, son of Edward Harris, DVM—word would spread around both towns that my father was no longer able to tend to their furry friends.

That truth will come out in a few more days, but on our terms, when we can formally announce the takeover and I can answer any client questions and assuage their fears and concerns.

Now, my mother rushes out the front door, chased by her two border collie mutts, black-and-white blurs of bounding paws and thumping tails. Ethan jumps out of the car, drops to the ground, and offers his face for kissing.

Being dogs, Elphaba and Galinda seize the chance to lick his cheeks, lips, and eyes.

"Make sure they clean your teeth too," I say as he laughs and falls to the grass, letting the dogs conduct a thorough tongue-lashing, like I bet Katrina did to him back in Florida.

"Girls, come now," my mum calls. "Off!"

"Too late." I shut the car door and head toward her. "He slathered himself with steak this morning."

"Well, he's won their allegiance for the rest of time, then," Mum says. Seconds later, Ethan pops up and gives her a hug. "Why, if it isn't my fifth-favorite grandson!" she declares, and he cracks up.

"Why can't I be first?" he asks.

She parks a hand on her hip, taps her chin, and seems to seriously consider his question. "Maybe you can, but you'll have to prove why you should be my favorite."

As the dogs circle his feet, he stares at her weather-worn face, her blonde hair gone silver, her blue eyes still bright and knowing. He has her genes, her fair complexion.

"What do I have to do to become your favorite?"

She peers around the yard. "You could start by mowing the lawn, then perhaps by weeding it."

I join them, thoroughly approving of her tough tactics. "You drive a hard bargain, Mum."

"Of course I do," she says, ruffling my hair.

I bend to pet the dogs, paying homage to their adorableness, then I point a finger at each one, and instantly they drop into proper sits.

"You're the dog wizard." Ethan sounds a little awed.

"And if I'm not, they should take away my license."

Mum flashes me a smile. "It's good to see you again, Liam."

"You saw us the other night," I point out.

"And I still like seeing you. Didn't anyone ever tell you to be nice to your mum?"

I roll my eyes. "I am nice. I'll show you how nice." I head to the back seat of the car, open the door, and reach inside to grab the bouquet of daisies.

I offer them to her, and she clasps her hand to her chest in delight and then takes the flowers. "I love them."

"They're from the woman next door," Ethan chimes in. He drops the mic after that and scampers into the house, the girls behind him, nipping at his feet.

"You've already met someone." My mother arches a *tell me all the details* brow.

"I've met my next-door neighbor."

"A woman?"

I stare off into the sky, bright and blue. "Yes, that does seem to be her gender, it's true."

"And you have your eye on her already?"

I chuckle, shaking my head—a lie, a big lie, a big, fat lie. "She's just my next-door neighbor. I don't know why you would say I have my eye on her."

"Because you've always had your eye on pretty women," she says.

Busted.

Her eyes shoot laser beams my way. "I'd like more grandchildren. So please get moving on that."

"Be grateful for what you have. I didn't even plan on giving you this one, but it worked out quite well, didn't it? Stop being so difficult," I tease, planting a quick kiss on her forehead. "Would you take a grand-dog instead?"

She swats my shoulder. "I swear, you and your sisters. Always so quick."

"So that's a yes to a rescue dog? Excellent."

Shaking her head, she deals me a stern stare. "And so when are you going to see this neighbor again?"

"I don't know. Probably all the time because she's my next-door neighbor." I look at my watch, then answer a little sheepishly, "Also, in about thirty minutes because we're going furniture shopping."

As I say that, a little zip of excitement whips through me. I hate shopping. I loathe shopping for furniture. And I detest IKEA. But I'm absolutely looking forward to going furniture shopping with January.

"Shopping," my mother says, as if it's a naughty word.

"It's just furniture shopping," I point out.

She gives me the satisfied smile that only a mother can dole out. "It's furniture shopping now, but in no time, she'll be knocked up and popping out more babies for me, okay?"

I hold up a hand. "I don't even think I can speak to you any longer." Then I sober as I shift to another subject, the reason I'm here. "How's Dad?"

Her mood cracks and sinks into sadness, but then she gamely tries to buoy up her emotions, pasting on a smile. "He's okay," she says in a chipper voice that sounds forced. "He's doing well enough. He had an appointment this morning to prep for the surgery next month."

"Is he ready?" That surgery is part of why I'm here. A big part.

She swallows roughly, but her voice is steady. "Some days he's all zen and accepts it. Other days he rages against the machine."

"And which one is he today?"

"Today he's simply happy that he's going to spend time with Ethan. We all enjoy that. And on that note, why don't you go see your lady friend for your IKEA date?"

"That's not what it is," I say. But I do pop inside and say hi to my father and bye to my son before I take off to meet my next-door neighbor for our definitely-not-a-date.

6

LIAM

January waits for me, leaning against the cab of her pink truck, looking sexy as sin and sweet as ice cream.

Because, damn. There's just something about a woman with ink who drives a pickup truck. She tosses the keys in the air and catches them, dealing me a serious gut-check sort of stare. "I've got supplies. Are you ready?"

I screw up the corner of my lips, tapping my chin. "Let's see." I pat the pocket of my jeans. "I've got some rations, a Leatherman, and a blueprint of the store that I found online."

She opens the door of her truck. "Perfect. I've got a camper stove too. Just in case."

"Are you a fan of camping?"

"I am. And judging from the look on your face, you're not?"

"What look exactly?"

She circles her finger, pointing at my face. "The

slight crinkle of your nose combined with just a touch of recoil."

"Sounds like a recipe." I pretend I'm reading a cookbook. "Start with a dollop of dislike, then toss in a dash of derision and a sprinkle of disdain. There you go."

A *well-done* grin glides across her face. "So, you *admit* you have a secret I Hate Camping face?"

"Oh. Was it a secret?" I ask with a deadpan expression. "According to you, it was readily apparent."

Shaking her head in amusement, she points to the passenger side. "Get in, radish-hating, camping-hating, comfy-furniture-hating neighbor."

Before I make my way around the truck, I hold open the door for her. "After you, furniture Sherpa."

She lifts her eyebrows approvingly as she hops into the cab. "Thank you. Very gentlemanly of you."

Yes, but it's also strategic. Gives me a chance to admire her backside. She has a great ass, and I enjoy lovely views.

So, I'm not *that* gentlemanly.

Closing the door behind her, I head to the passenger side, get in, and snap on my seat belt.

I peer into the bed of the truck as if I'm checking out her survival supplies. The bed of her truck is actually empty—pristine too, as if newly cleaned. "Is there a tent that goes along with this camper stove of yours? In case we're stuck overnight?"

She scoffs as she turns on the engine. "Don't be silly. We can just curl up in a king-size bed and catch our Zs in the bedroom section if we want."

Oh, did she just go there, to flirty and dirty land? I believe she did. And I do believe I liked it.

Maybe too much though.

That's the trouble. She's sarcastic, friendly, helpful, and sexy as hell, but also completely ineligible. I have to remember she's my next-door neighbor. She's exactly who I can't pursue in my efforts to find Mrs. Right. To provide for Ethan what I was lucky enough to have growing up—a stable, steady family.

Even though we moved continents, even though it was hard as hell at first, I was lucky to have two parents who looked out for me, who talked to me, who gave me everything I needed to become the person I wanted to be.

Now I want to give my son everything I experienced, and I know he misses having a mum.

But that won't be January.

She won't be Mrs. Right.

She can only be Ms. Next Door.

Anything else would be foolish. Because if we didn't work out, she'd be a stone's throw away. That would be awkward. Possibly uncomfortable. Potentially as agonizing as trying to use a PC when you're used to a Mac.

And there's the kid factor. Ethan could get attached, and that spells trouble too.

He doesn't need another loss in his life.

That makes my neighbor thoroughly off-limits.

First things first—once I settle into my new home and new job, I can start this whole dating-for-keeps business in earnest, and approach it with stealth so that Ethan doesn't meet her before we're solid as a rock.

Which means I'm simply going to embrace having a next-door neighbor who's fun, easygoing, and tempting as hell.

That's especially true as she stretches her arm across the back of my seat and twists to look behind her, giving me a view of the sparrows on her right arm. They fly down her shoulder, soar across her biceps, and curl around to below her elbow. The ink is delicate, feminine, and impossible to look away from.

What do they mean? Why did she get them? And does she have more ink that's hidden from my view?

I shake away my wayward thoughts. "How do you want to tackle this shopping expedition today? Besides forging our own path and refusing to be funneled through the endless retail labyrinth?"

"I have my plan of attack. I wrote a task list. It's like a schedule and has water breaks and even snack times," she says as she puts the truck in drive.

"Are we talking Pirate's Booty–type snacks, or more like apple slices and peanut butter?"

"Please. After yesterday, I'm never giving you fresh food again. It's Pirate's Booty all the way for you, mister." She turns down the next road. "And don't forget, if we get lost or confused in the store or we just can't find our way out, we can always call for help."

I rub my finger against my ear. "What did you just say? Call for help?"

She groans. "Oh, you're one of *those* guys. The kind who doesn't believe in asking for help."

I thump my chest, playing up the stereotype to egg her on. "I'm a man. I'm not allowed to ask for help."

"Anyone can ask for help," she says, a touch worked up and a touch adorable.

"Then it's a good thing you'll be there in case someone needs to do it." Laughing will ruin the pretense that this is a sticking point for me, so I keep a straight face.

She arches a dubious brow. "Would you really not ask for help? What's so wrong with that? Nice guys ask for help when they need it."

I roll my eyes, continuing the ruse. "Great. Now you think I'm a nice guy. Just fucking great."

"Don't put words in my mouth. I didn't say you were nice. I asked if you'd really refuse to ask for help."

"By your logic, nice guys ask for help. So if you expect me to do it, you must think I'm . . ." I curl my lip in exaggerated disdain. "Nice."

She glances my way, a sly little smirk on her pretty face. "You're saying you want to be a mean guy?"

"I'm saying even nice guys don't want to be called nice guys."

"So, you don't want to be a mean guy, you don't want to be a nice guy, and you're prepared to wander forever through IKEA rather than ask for help?"

I'm losing the battle against laughter. "You're really good at talking, aren't you?"

She flashes me a victorious grin. "It's kind of my thing."

I laugh, enjoying the moment. "I confess—I'm one

hundred percent fine with asking for help. But it is my goal to make it out of the store without needing to. And I always try to exceed my goals."

With a smile, she turns on the blinker and says, "Here's to exceeding goals today, then."

As she turns onto the highway, I gesture toward the hood of her truck, making conversation. "Big fan of pink?"

She turns to me briefly, her eyes glimmering. "I am. I'm all about leaning into it."

I laugh at the way she put that. "Leaning into the whole lady carpenter thing?"

Her brows shoot up, like she can't believe I said that. "*Thing?* A lady carpenter thing? First of all, it's not a thing. It's a profession."

Perhaps I didn't phrase that the best way. Before I can backtrack, she adds, "Unless you want me to start referring to you as Liam the Male Vet. Should I do that?"

She's called me out so delightfully that I have to laugh. "May I humbly suggest Liam the Male Vet Who Just Put His Foot in His Mouth?"

She tsks, but with humor. "How *does* it fit in there? You managed the whole shoe in up to the ankle."

I pretend to talk with my mouth full. "Not much room for Pirate's Booty."

"You don't deserve booty of any kind," she says. I choke, and her smirk turns into another *I win* grin.

But joking aside, I take a breath to explain and make proper amends. "The way I said that was unfortunate, and I'm sorry. I meant it more as a compliment—the uniqueness of being a woman in your field. The coolness of it. I get the sense that you embrace it for what it is, with the pink hammer and truck and all that. And really, I should have said, 'I bet you're great with a hammer.'"

"Points for not going with the obvious." At my inquiring look, she quotes, "'I bet you like to get nailed.'"

"Ouch." I grimace in sympathy. "Please tell me no one says that."

She laughs. "No, they don't, actually, because I know how to work a power saw."

I shudder, raising my hands as if to ward her off.

"Anyway," she says. "Nice recovery. Very well done." She takes a beat, then adds, "Maybe you're a mildly nice guy."

"There is nothing mild about me," I say with narrowed eyes and a deliberate growl that makes her laugh.

"Actually, I have to agree. You're not milquetoast at all."

"I've always aspired to *not* be milquetoast."

"You're exceeding that goal too. And to answer your question, yes, I love pink. I'm going to do a whole accent wall in my house in pink now that I finally can."

There's a story in the way she ends that sentence. Before I can ask about it, she tosses a question to me instead. "What do you think of Duck Falls so far?"

"I actually went to high school one town over. In Lucky Falls," I say.

She glances briefly at me in surprise, then says, "I want to hear all about that."

The rest of the drive, we chat about how I came to America as a teen, then again in my late twenties, and I figure there'll be time on the way back to learn about her, and why she's finally able to indulge in that accent wall when she couldn't before.

7

JANUARY

The store is forty-five miles away from Duck Falls.

Normally, I'm all about efficiency. As a single mom and a small business owner trying to make a dent in a male-dominated field, I don't have a lot of time to mess around. And I don't have a lot of time for myself.

Hell, self-care is something I have to schedule, my phone beeping with nightly reminders to lotion up my feet with coconut body cream. Then I'll drag a pair of fluffy socks out of the drawer and pull them on for bed, all while Alva and I text about her day at the salon and mine tooling around town.

That's the extent of my maintenance routine—texting my best friend while making sure my feet don't get all cracked.

I don't have time to amble around—by my lonesome, or with anyone else.

But Wednesday's off with Alva's daughter, Audrey, working on YouTube videos where they sample quirky food like grape gum and bento boxes.

Meanwhile, I'm enjoying all forty-five inefficient miles in my neighbor's company, as he tells me about going to high school in neighboring Lucky Falls, before he returned to England for university and vet school, then came back to the States in his late twenties. Which explains why his British accent is still so yummy and . . . *British*.

"So, you were going to high school in Lucky Falls while I was in Duck Falls," I remark. "Small world."

"Are you thinking we would have run into each other at the football games?"

I toss him a doubtful look. "Why do I think you didn't attend football games?"

"Are you casting aspersions on my sportiness, or lack thereof?"

I flick the fingers of my right hand at him as I drive. "I am indeed. Aspersions cast."

He huffs, folding his arms over his chest. "Fine. I didn't go to football games."

"Neither did I," I say with a wide grin, offering a palm for a high five.

He unfolds his arms and smacks back. "Is this a geeks unite thing? Or science geeks, to be precise."

I laugh. "I was more into woodshop and theater tech. So maybe it's more like woodshop tomboys and science geeks unite."

"All right. Fair enough. Tomboys and geeks. So that explains why we never ran into each other. But what year did you graduate?"

I tell him, and he reciprocates. The arithmetic is easy to figure. "You're thirty-nine?" I ask.

"*So old.* And you're . . . twenty-two?"

"Is that your way of making up for the lady carpenter thing?"

"Did it work?"

"Perhaps," I say, then I whisper, "Even though I'm thirty-seven."

"Yes, I figured that out, since we were two years apart in school."

"A math geek too," I say dryly. "So impressive."

A little later, we arrive at IKEA, where I put on my most serious face. "I wrote a list. I have a plan. I'm ready."

His brow knits in confusion. "You planned out what I need to buy?"

"I did," I say, owning it. "That's part of the house-warming gift. It didn't seem like something you wanted to do."

He brings his hand to his chest and sighs dramatically. "You are an angel of mercy."

"Just wait until your sink clogs, or your dryer goes on the fritz. You'll elevate me to goddess status when I can come fix it for you."

"I'm promoting you right now just for offering, January." As we march into the store, a determined spring in both our steps, he lifts a brow. "Speaking of January, how is it that you and your daughter have such similar names?"

"Well, it may have something to do with the fact she's my daughter and I got to name her."

He laughs as we step onto the escalator. "I meant, was it as deliberate as it seems, you being named after a month and her after a day of the week? But I suppose that's my answer."

"I always liked the name Wednesday. I suppose I don't mind, either, when things match."

"You say that like it's a confession. Like matching things are near and dear to your heart."

"They are. Wine and chocolate, coffee and cream, hammer and nail. And now, January and Wednesday."

"If she has children, do you think they'll be named Minute or Second?"

At the top of the escalator, we turn into the linens section. "Please. Don't be silly. If she gives me a grandchild, I'll insist on the name Five O'clock."

"Because that's the best time of day?"

"My favorite time of the day is actually ten at night." I slow my pace, tapping my chin. "No, probably eleven. I love the quiet of nighttime."

"You're a night owl," he says, musing on this newly learned fact.

"I am. And what about you? Are you a morning person?"

"What do you think?" He flashes me a grin. The way the man alternates between droll and cheery is kind of adorable.

"You seem like a morning person."

"And why do you say that?" he asks as he follows me through the kitchenware.

"I think it's because you have this sort of upbeat personality."

He exaggerates a grimace. "Don't tell anybody. I

really want to keep up my reputation as a ne'er-do-well or a curmudgeon."

"You're doing a horrible job of pretending to be either of those."

"I'm working on it. In the meantime, like I said, don't tell anyone."

I bring my finger to my lips, swearing secrecy, then I focus on the shopping list.

After all, I am a woman on a mission. A couch mission.

We make our way through housewares, stopping only at an adorable steel trash can that's so cute I have to grab a pink one.

"Penchant for pink," I explain.

"And pink trash cans are irresistible?"

"Clearly."

He holds out his arm, silently offering to carry it. I hand it over, thanking him. Next, we come to shelves and bins full of pillows, and I slow then stop because . . . pillows.

I wiggle my fingers at them. "Must have pillows."

He lifts a brow, looking perplexed. "You need pillows?"

"I *want* pillows," I correct. "Don't let the whole tomboy vibe throw you. I am big on pillows."

"What's not to like? They're soft and fluffy, and they help lubricate the path to sleep."

A laugh springs from my chest. "I don't really think of pillows as lubrication."

"Ah, that's an issue, then. Pillows are absolutely a

lubricant. I highly recommend them for easing into a good night's sleep."

"I sleep quite well."

"Do you sleep on pillows?"

"I do sleep on pillows."

"Then the lubricant is doing its job, isn't it?"

"Fine, fine," I surrender with a laugh. "You got me there."

"You are the girliest tomboy," he remarks as I grab a sparkly purple one.

"I am."

We go to the couches, and my gears start whirring. I recommend a dark-blue one for him. He approves it instantly. Tables next—I suggest a simple wood one for him, and he says, "I'll get it."

He's easy, so easy that when we reach the chairs, I can't resist patting a strange egg-shaped one with a pull-down shade so you can hide inside it. "And this seems like your style. You can use it as a chair fort."

His brow lifts. "Just the thing every man needs."

"Of course. Didn't you see *GQ*'s list of 'Top Ten Things a Manly Man Needs'? Scotch, an old-fashioned shave kit, and a chair fort."

Stroking his chin, he makes a show of thinking it over. "Afraid I missed that one. I trust your judgment, but I'd better try it out to be sure."

He crouches and inserts himself into the egg, then tugs the cover down, turning the chair into a kind of capsule.

Laughter threads through me. "Is it everything you've ever wanted in a chair?"

"My God, this is bloody fantastic. Give me a book, and I'll never leave."

When he slides open the cover, I have my phone ready and snap a pic.

"I can only presume that you're going to file that under *future blackmail material*?"

"It's like you know me so well already."

We move along, choosing a different chair, a simple one that's durable too.

We head to the nearest clerk at the checkout, handing over the tags for the items. "Do you want home delivery for these?" he asks.

"Absolutely," Liam says.

"And would you like assembly?"

Liam says yes, but I override him. "He doesn't."

He shoots me a look. "I can put a dog's leg back together, but I can't assemble a chair from instructions. And see, I'm not afraid to ask for help when I need it."

I grin at his honesty, but assure him, "I want to do it. It's part of the housewarming gift. Just another perk of living next door to a carpenter goddess."

"Thank you. That would be amazing," he says to me, then finishes with the clerk. He also insists on buying my pillows and trash can, and I let him.

As he grabs the bag of pillows, my stomach rumbles. Liam doesn't pretend he doesn't hear, which seems in keeping with his straightforward nature. "You should let me feed you," he says.

"I won't object to that." We duck into the store café, where I grab a salad, he grabs a sandwich, and we find a table next to a family. The mom is offering a meatball to the little blonde toddler across from her, the girl opening her mouth wide as the mom airplanes the food into it. The dad—or so I assume—plates a scoop of mashed potatoes for the young boy across from him. Like a seagull, the boy dips a fork in, declares *yum*, and his dad laughs.

They look tired, but happy.

Across from me, Liam looks contemplative as he takes a bite of his sandwich, studying me as he chews. "So, at the risk of being blunt—is Wednesday's father dead? Did he pass away? Is he out of the picture?"

I put down my fork and wipe the napkin across my mouth. "You are straightforward, aren't you?"

"Yes, I try to be. Does that bother you?"

I shake my head. "I like it. Most people aren't."

"Why tiptoe when you can be blunt? As I like to say."

"Words to live by," I agree. I set my hands on the table, thinking about where to begin the story. It's not one I'm ashamed of. It's my own, and there's no reason not to tell him.

"Wednesday was an oopsie with my college boyfriend on graduation night. Things were sort of petering out with us, but then I found out I was pregnant. And so, we got married, because that's what you do. We stayed together for a while, but it was mostly out of obligation."

I wish things had been different with Vince, but it was never really in the cards. He and I tried; we definitely tried. But there was no spark, no deep, soulful connection. We were partners in parenting, and partners in navigating life. We weren't partners in love.

"A few years ago, we made plans to amicably separate. He met someone else almost immediately and moved to Texas to marry her. He's not terribly involved with Wednesday—just sees her during the summers." I smile, and it's genuine. I want my daughter to spend time with her father. "He's a good man who loves his kid. Just not the right man for me, and I wasn't right for him."

He smiles softly. "It's kind of amazing that you say that."

I snort. "Not really."

"Lovely sound of derision, by the way."

"Thanks. I've been working on it for years, hoping someone would notice."

"Achievement unlocked." Then he returns to his point. "It's amazing because so many people talk about their ex like they're the worst person in the universe. 'He was a total twat.' 'He didn't appreciate me.' 'She was borderline insane.' 'She clung to me like static to laundry,'" he says, and I laugh at the last one. "But it takes a lot to be honest and admit that you weren't right for each other."

"We weren't, and trust me, I wish we had been. I wish it had been love, hearts, and lots of banging on the kitchen counter like my friend Alva and her hubs."

He laughs deeply and wiggles his brow. "So your friend is a kitchen fucker?"

It's my turn to crack up. "Yes. Or at least she likes to tell me about all the places she and Marcos get it on. Like the staircase, or the bathroom sink, or the storage trunk in the attic."

He arches one brow. "Storage trunk in the attic?"

"Yeah, I don't quite get that one either. I decided not to ask."

"Some things you may just not want to know."

"They were high school sweethearts, and their first time was in the garage or something, so maybe it was nostalgic." I smile, happy for my still-very-much-in-love best friend. "But Vince and I didn't have that long-term bond. When it ended, I think we were both relieved."

"So, it's you and Wednesday against the world over there in Duck Falls?"

"It is, and I like it that way."

He pauses for a sip of his iced tea. "You seem pretty tough. Pretty good at holding your own."

"Thanks. I think we are too. It's freeing now that it's just us. I can focus on my business, on my kid. I don't have to worry about a man," I say, relieved all over again. I'm so glad that my time is mine, my chores are for me. Glad, too, that I learned how to say *fuck it* to worries that had plagued me for years.

"The business is growing?"

"Yes," I say with a smile. "Just last night, after I delivered the hated vegetables, I finished fixing Betty Juniper's spice rack. She lives down the street. And I'm hoping to snag a deal to do some work for Nina Clawson at the boba tea shop, but the competition is fierce."

"You're fierce. I wouldn't want to go up against you," he says.

"Thanks." I appreciate the compliment, though I don't tell him how long it took me to get my act together work-wise, to figure out what I actually wanted to do for a living. That I'd puttered around as a handywoman for my father's construction company for years before I figured out that I wanted to run my own business. He's now retired, having given some of his company's assets to me when I started.

But old habits die hard, and it took me that long to drown out the soundtrack in my head: *What if you fail, what if it doesn't work, what if you suck at it?*

Lowering the volume on that voice took ages and lots of tough love from my best friend, but that's not what this conversation is about.

"What about you and your son?" Picking up my fork again, I take a bite of my salad as I shift the conversation back to him and his family.

"Ah. It's kind of an interesting story." He glances at a man pushing a stroller past us, who snags a table a few feet away.

"Interesting how?"

"Interesting in the fact that I didn't even know I had a kid until he was almost seven."

He's right. That's got to be a helluva story.

8

———

JANUARY

Liam makes that admission in a light tone, with a "told you it was unusual" self-awareness. It must be a complicated situation, though, and I normally like someone who can poke a little fun at himself. But not if it's a front to hide pain.

"That definitely sounds like a story you don't hear every day." I leave him an opening, and when he doesn't fill it, I say, "You don't have to tell me what happened, but I'd like to know."

He leans back in the chair, dragging his hand across his chin. He sighs, but it's not so much that he's deciding whether to speak but more like where to start. "Ten years ago, I had—and this is not the unusual part of the story—a one-night stand. She was from England, but lived in Florida. She was in town for a conference I was attending too. We connected over a drinks thing and ended up at my place—which she left at two in the morning. Just slipped out of my apartment and out of my life. No 'look me up if you're ever in West Palm

Beach.' Didn't even stay for breakfast. It was seven years before I heard from her again."

I fear that the story is heading in an unhappy direction, and my heart sinks as Liam's expression shifts.

His lips go straight, his brown eyes brimming with sadness. "She literally showed up on my doorstep. Rang the bell. Told me she had terminal cancer, no family, and a child who was mine."

A cold twist of sympathy pulls at me, thinking of all those tragic things falling on someone at once, especially on a child like Liam's son. "I'm so sorry, Liam. That's so hard for everyone involved."

"Thank you. I appreciate that," he says. No teasing or sarcasm now. He takes my words as seriously as I mean them, and his thanks is just as earnest. "Yes, it was rough on so many levels. I barely knew her, but my heart would have gone out to a total stranger in her situation. Alone, sick, and with a kid—my kid. We did DNA tests to verify that Ethan was my son, got the legalities settled, and she stayed with a friend in New York for the last few weeks of her life while Ethan came to live with me. I helped out some, and he visited her. Not much longer after that, she passed away. Everything was quite sudden." He blows out a long stream of air as he brings the story back to the present. "That's how I suddenly became parent to a seven-year-old I had no idea existed."

I shake my head, processing Ethan's story. Liam's story. "How did he deal with it, losing his mother and then making such a dramatic change?"

"He was devastated. He cried himself to sleep almost

every night, understandably. And I didn't know how the hell to help him deal with so many losses—his mother, and his home . . . his whole life."

The tightness in his voice gives me a window into how frustrated and helpless Liam must have felt. He doesn't linger there though. "Fortunately, I'm close with my mum and dad, so Mum came East and spent some time with us. Her sister, my Aunt Jane, lives in New York too. They all helped me figure it out, and I found a great child psychologist who helped Ethan process his grief."

Liam flashes a quick, relieved grin. "I'm lucky—he came through the other side and is remarkably well-adjusted. We get on great, and we're thick as thieves now. But it makes me wonder all the time how life would have been with him at two, three, four . . ." He drifts off, turning wistful, maybe a bit sad, even, longing for the time missed. The years they didn't have together.

"You would have loved each other back then like you do now," I say, not sure if that will make him feel better or miss the time even more. "But I don't think your connection is weakened by not having those years. You were there when it mattered."

He shoots me a soft smile. "I'd like to think so. But I'll never know." He sighs, as though recalibrating, before moving on. "In any case, here we are now. It's the strangest thing—three and a half years ago, I didn't know he existed, but now he's my whole world in one pint-size person," he says, wrapping up the story with a happy ending, full of awe and joy.

"Sounds like parenthood to me," I say with a smile.

He deals me one in return. "Yeah, I suppose it is. I don't have as much experience as you, but I'm learning."

"From what I've seen, you're doing a great job," I say. "I'm glad Ethan's mom was able to find you, and that you could give him the family that he needed."

"Me too. It changed everything. And at first it was such a shock I didn't know if I could handle it. But now I can't imagine life without him."

"Kids have a way of doing that, don't they?"

"That they do," he says as he surveys the café teeming with shopped-out young families with babies and toddlers and tykes. "That they definitely do."

"And now, is it still you and him against the world?"

"I suppose it is, but I hope not forever," he says, taking another bite of his sandwich, looking a little lost in thought.

Those are words that make me think too. *Not forever.*

Do they mean what they seem?

That even though he's definitely single, he might not be for long.

"So, you're looking to settle down?"

He offers me a sheepish smile. "Yes. I've dated, had my fun, and it doesn't really appeal to me anymore. I'm almost forty, and at this point, yeah, I'd like to find someone to settle down with. Be a family. Have what my parents have. It was lovely to grow up with both my parents, see them support each other, love each other. Even through my dark, rebellious days as a teen, I knew I had them. I'd like Ethan to have that same security."

I gulp at his directness, but mostly from the rarity of

a man coming right out and saying he wants something that many men won't admit to wanting.

"You want more kids, then?" My throat is unexpectedly dry.

His shrug says he wouldn't mind more munchkins at all. His gaze travels around the café as if he's saying, *Yes, let's order the mac and cheese feast like that table over there,* or *Check out those parents slicing up lingonberry pancakes for their kiddos.*

He returns his eyes to me, startlingly vulnerable when he admits, "If it happened, I wouldn't object. I'd like more. I like kids." He takes a beat, then, in the most earnest tone I've ever heard, says, "And I'd like to be there every day for my kid."

My heart bangs loudly in my chest and, at the same time, tries to flee to a corner to hide. The sentiment is wildly endearing. It would have hooked me like a trout if I were single in my twenties.

My God, if I'd met him then and he'd said those things—I'd have flung myself at him and begged him to take me to bed and MAKE BABIES WITH ME RIGHT THAT INSTANT.

Heck, I'd have grabbed him and tugged him into the chair fort to procreate.

But with a teen who's entering her sophomore year of high school, with a business I'm finally getting off the ground, with a life I'm finally living on my own terms— one that took more than a decade to realize—I don't want to start over.

I don't want that.

At all.

I'm not in the market for more babies, for another pregnancy.

And for a second—no, for several seconds—my heart is an anchor, weighing me down with a heaviness I shouldn't feel.

After all, the man lives next door to me. That's reason enough to shove all these errant tingles into a metaphorical closet and ignore them until they go away.

Surely they'll go away soon.

These tingles come from airborne lust particles. From the yummy, clean, woodsy scent of him. From the empirically handsome face he happens to possess.

That's all. He's easy on the eyes.

Nothing more.

I'll adjust, get used to it, and I won't think twice about the flip my heart executes when he flashes those big brown eyes at me.

I fasten on a smile. "Since you want a family, I'd say it's a good thing we moved you away from the man-cave furniture," I say, doing my best to keep the mood light. I sweep my arm out to indicate the store and the mission of the day. "You're getting a whole new look for the settling-down phase of your life."

"No more bachelor pad furniture, thanks to your help." He takes a beat, then with serious eyes, he asks, "What about you? Any settling down in your future? More kids?"

I gasp, shrinking back. "More kids? No. I'm still working up the nerve to adopt a cat. With my kid a mere three years away from college"—I stop to pat my belly—"I'm good with keeping the shop closed."

"Cat, kid . . . What's the difference, really?" he asks, holding his hands out as if weighing both options. "And when will this cat come into your life?"

"Ripley?"

His forehead knits in confusion. "What's that?"

"I'm going to name my future cat Ripley."

"Not Every Other Week or 1982?"

I stare sharp knives at him. "Ripley, as in the badass alien hunter from four flicks."

"Do you want your future cat to hunt aliens?"

"Look, if aliens are coming, that's a damn good time to have an alien-hunting cat."

"True. I like a woman who plans ahead," he says. "When will we meet Ripley?"

I shrug. Took me long enough to start my business—I bet it takes me longer to commit to a pet. "It could be anywhere from three days to ten years. And what about you? When are you going to start dating?"

The question comes out sticky, like each word is glued to my tongue.

But what the hell?

He can date.

He *should* date.

"Soon. Very soon."

"Online, I presume?"

"Tinder, here I come." He sounds excited, but there's some trepidation too. "Once I get settled in at my dad's practice, I'll start up a *LovesToCookShowerYouwithGiftsandGiveFootRubs* profile. Think that's a good dating profile name?"

"I mean, maybe?" I tease. "The only edit, I suppose, would be *AlsoGoodinBed*."

Maybe that was too flirty. Maybe I shouldn't have said that.

"Ohhh," he says with a sly grin. "You suppose I'm good in bed?"

My mouth falls open as a flush creeps across my cheeks. I hold up my hands, not wanting to touch that one, even though I started it.

He taps my toe with his. "C'mon. You think I'm probably good in bed. I give off good-in-bed vibes, don't I?"

And the flush turns into flames. "I'm pleading the fifth."

"Look, you can sense the truth. I get it. And let's just be up-front, like you were about the furniture." He leans a little closer, dropping his voice. "You're completely right. But . . ." His tone goes low and smoky as he shoots me a dangerous look. "We can call it *GreatinBed*."

A myriad of risqué thoughts gallop through my brain, runaway horses heating me up. I have got to wrest control of this conversation. So I take a breath, imagine the air clearing away filthy thoughts of saddling him up for a wild mustang ride, and say, "You came to the right town. The women will be lining up for a guy who cooks, loves animals, and is great in bed."

"That's all I've ever wanted," he teases.

* * *

As we leave, I'm keenly aware of a few key facts.

One, I'm glad he moved next door.

Two, he already feels like a friend.

Three, he is going to be such a hot commodity in Duck Falls.

Later that evening, Alva, though not in the market, texts me to get a jump on everyone else for the details. She asks how the shopping trip went, but I know what she really means, because she follows up with a GIF of a doe-eyed celebrity, batting her lashes and saying, *Tell me more.*

January: He's everything all the women in town whispered he'd be.

Alva: You lucky bitch. You get to live next door to him.

January: How does that make me lucky exactly?

Alva: Because you can just climb out your window when you want to bang him.

January: Yes, of course. I'll sneak across the front lawn barefoot in my nightgown and get some lovin'.

Alva: Now you're talking. Anyway, so . . . what's next?

January: With Liam? What's next is we are neighbors, nothing more.

Alva: *sigh* I was hoping for a good story. Make one up for me, will ya?

January: Does that mean fifteen years of marriage and three kids is getting a bit dull?

Alva: On the contrary! I was hoping your story would be all I needed to jump my hubs after a long day. And hey, it worked. K, thanks, bye.

January: I didn't even tell you a story!

Alva: I made one up in my head, and now I'm going to pretend I'm sixteen again and sneaking across the lawn to bang my high school sweetheart.

January: I hate you and your perfect love life.

Alva: Sorry, not sorry! Love you madly too. See you at B&B night next week!

January: Board games and booze. I never miss it.

Alva: And I never miss sex with the hubs. Gonna go chase me some Os!

I close the text thread with my bestie, glad she's still happy, glad she's still in love and lust with her guy after all these years.

Glad for her, since I don't want that for myself.

Even though I am keenly aware of a fourth fact concerning Liam.

I'm the slightest bit jealous of the women he'll date, and the slightest bit annoyed that I'm not in the market.

Because I'm absolutely not shopping. Not at all. Not one bit.

I've only now gotten through a divorce and come out on the other side of sadness.

I won't tango with my next-door neighbor, a man who wants more kids.

I resolve to be the best of friends with him.

And only friends.

9

LIAM

A few days later, while Ethan is still asleep, I hop on my bike at the crack of dawn and ride.

The sun climbs above the hilly terrain of this edge-of-wine-country town, warming my shoulders as I crest the final slope of a long, hard climb. Reaching the top, I flash back to my conversation at IKEA with January.

As the glorious descent calls out to me, my legs and lungs crying for relief, my mind zooms in on the possibilities of dating.

After all, dating isn't new to me.

I enjoyed my twenties in New York, thank you very much. My early thirties too. And my mid-thirties. Hell, it's not as if I stopped dating when Ethan appeared on my doorstep. Scheduling became more complicated, but I still went out from time to time, enjoying the city—dining in new restaurants, attending ball games, checking out the top-ten small-batch ice cream shops.

Ice cream is a priority.

Love?

Not so much up until now.

I came close a few times, or at least I think I did.

I'm pretty sure it was love with my college girl-friend, Anna. Though I might be basing that mostly on the stepped-barefoot-on-a-Lego pain I felt when she dumped me.

My first broken heart had me wallowing in misery so deep that my dad took it upon himself to comfort me, assuring me that it wouldn't last forever and that someday I wouldn't be sad over that girl.

And it was true. I stopped being sad about Anna long before I stopped feeling outraged that she left me for a long-haired, flannel-wearing bloke who fronted for a band called Tirade, which sounded like Soundgarden imitating Alice in Chains imitating Pearl Jam imitating Nirvana.

And Anna thought Tirade was fantastic.

Who was this girl? Had she always had such horrible taste in music? Had she only pretended to like the bands I'd introduced her to, bands like Snow Patrol, Radio-head, and the Foo Fighters?

So maybe it was less of a broken heart and more of an existential crisis.

Later in my twenties, there was Brittani with an *I*, who ran a dog rescue in the city. I handled all of their spays and neuters. We bonded over a love of animals and sex with an O, but eventually realized we had nothing to discuss outside of bed besides dogs and cats.

There was Stella, a baker I met through my friend Summer. It started as a match made in sugary heaven—she needed a taste-tester for her recipes, and I needed calories to burn as I trained for the centuries I was riding. We fell into friendship and wound up the best of mates. In fact, I took my next girlfriend as my date to her wedding.

Now, as I fly down this California hill on my bike, hugging the curves of the road, I look back at my serial monogamy without regret. There are no dreadful mistakes in my romantic past. No clingers or crazies, no one who cheated, stole, or banged my best mate.

Sure, I haven't met *the one*, but I'm fortunate to have met plenty of women I liked. And if I managed that without trying, then the search for Ms. Right should be a piece of cake.

Ethan and I both long for a family, but I'm not scouting for a mother replacement for him. I'm looking for me, dating for me, because I want what I haven't found yet.

What my parents have.

What my sister has.

I see it in clients who come in as couples, doting over the brand-new tortoiseshell kitten or floppy-eared puppy they've acquired, doting on each other as they take the next step in their togetherness.

It's there in the bookstore when I spot a pair checking out books, showing each other things they know will make them think, or laugh, or just enjoy.

In the park with my son, I see how the other parents are with each other, holding hands as the kids play. Love has been on my mind a lot since Ethan came into my life.

I make my way home, cycling past emerald-green

grass and acres of grapes, and let myself imagine that kind of life. And as I slow my pace at the end of my ride, turning onto Mallard Lane, I let those thoughts fade away, shelving them for now. There will be time later to tackle all those wishes.

I roll past the houses on my street, which still feels a little like a foreign land. But it's a map I'm beginning to learn. My yellow home comes into view, and beyond that is January's light-blue one with the unmistakable ladybug mailbox in the front.

There's something even better there too—my neighbor.

I stop my bike in front of my house, dismount, and wheel it to hers, where I lean it against the white picket fence. January is in her garden, picking green beans, it looks like. She shoots me a devilish look as she snaps one off and waggles it in my direction. I make the sign of the cross to ward it off, and she cracks up and climbs to her feet, swiping her hair away from her face.

She pushes her sunglasses on top of her head, and I take mine off too, tucking them in the neck of my bike shirt before I undo my helmet and rest it on the handlebars.

"How can a vet hate veggies? Doctors shouldn't hate veggies," she says.

"I'm a DVM."

"Same idea."

"It's not the same at all. And actually, most of my patients detest green beans too."

She raises her eyebrows. "So it rubbed off on you—a dog's dislike of veggies?"

I smile. "Seems to be the case."

A wicked glint crosses her eyes. "I should make my sautéed green beans for you. I bet you'd change your mind."

I rub my ear. "Did you say cupcakes? If you did, I would be delighted to try them."

She ignores my comment. "They're so delicious, Liam," she says, sounding so enticing that she almost tricks me into thinking I could like the veggie dish. "A little garlic, a little olive oil, a little salt and pepper—I swear, they melt in your mouth."

I stroke my chin and hum out loud. "I feel like you have a fundamental misunderstanding of what happens when vegetables go past your lips. Chocolate melts. Green beans don't."

She laughs, dragging a hand through her hair, which drifts on the breeze like she's advertising air or water or some other essential. "I promise—you won't be able to resist them," she says, still trying to reel me in. It's not the green beans I can't seem to resist though—it's this beauty with the spray of freckles and bright blue eyes.

"Try me," I say, then toss out a counter-challenge. "But I guarantee you won't be able to resist my brownies."

"You're a baker?" she asks, sounding like I just announced I'm an astronaut.

"I'm pretty good in the kitchen." I smirk. "You should see what I can do with a KitchenAid."

"Wait." She holds up a hand to pause the conversation. "You said you love to cook, but there's a difference between enjoying something and being good at it."

"Oh, I'm good." I lean in closer and whisper like it's a dirty secret, "The best."

"Wow. Good in bed *and* good in the kitchen? How is that possible?"

I give an *if you've got it, flaunt it* shrug. "Like I said, I'm a hot commodity. Oh, wait—*you're* the one who said that."

She laughs. "I did say that. Speaking of, when does the great dating escapade begin?" She taps her wrist, but there's no watch there. Still, *ticktock.*

"Soon. Actually, I guess I could start today. I suppose I should get on the apps, at least."

She shoos me away. "Get moving, then, Liam."

But I don't leave, and I don't think she wants me to either, judging from the smile she's sporting.

The one that matches mine.

We stand there for a moment, and neither of us says anything. The silence feels awkward, like perhaps we ought to fill it. Maybe with questions—like the kind I'd ask if I invited her over for dinner. We'd cook, crack open a bottle of wine, and I'd find out what she likes most about living here, what makes her happy, what makes her sad, what makes her tick.

But I don't ask any of those things, because that's not the conversation we're having or going to have.

Instead, I return to her other question, answering as best I can. "I suppose I better make that *GoodinBed* profile tonight."

"Are you ready to take the plunge?"

Am I? That's a damn good question.

"As ready as I can be." I pat where the pockets would

be on my bike shorts, as if checking for my keys and wallet. "Small talk? Check. Questions about the other person? Check. Skin as thick as a rhino's? Check."

Chuckling, she shakes her head. "Ability to make a rhino sound both appealing and off-putting? Check."

"I guess I am ready, then." I try to imagine what this great dating escapade will look like as I admit to the ladies of the apps that I hate green beans and love brownies and enjoy a good audiobook on science and live for long, punishing bike rides that make my thighs scream and clear my mind of whatever is weighing on it.

A hard ride is blissful oblivion.

Except today, for some reason, with the trip down relationship memory lane. But thoughts of love and dating have dug in deep, and they're hard to bat away when they're tied to my plans for the near future.

"You're brave, Liam," she says, her voice kind, almost like a gentle caress.

"How's that?" I ask.

"For putting yourself out there." I look for sarcasm, but it seems to be a true and earnest compliment.

I like the sound of it. I like the feel of it. "You think so?"

"I do. It takes courage to be honest about what you want, like you were with me at IKEA." Her smile is so warm, so inviting. It's like the blue sky above.

But am I braver than her? Than this woman standing in her garden, who's been equally forthright? "You're honest too. About what you want, what you don't want."

She simply shrugs and shakes her head. "I don't

know. It seems easier to shut down an idea than to open up to one. Is it courageous to say I'm not interested?"

I nod, and keep nodding, like the movement of my head can underscore the truth of my words. "Yes. I think it is. Knowing and saying what you don't want is just as brave. Maybe more."

She lifts her chin, looking a little bit proud, and taps me on the shoulder in playful acknowledgment. "Then, we're both brave."

"We'll be brave together, just in different ways."

"Yes. I'll hold down Fort Single, and you trek into the dating wilds," she says, sweeping her arm out wide as if to indicate the rocky terrain I'm about to traverse.

Rocky indeed. "Sounds like a plan."

* * *

That evening, I find a white Pyrex dish on my porch with a note affixed to it. I unfold the paper, an unexpected warmth bursting in my chest chased by a widening smile as I read, "I promise *these will melt in your mouth. They are a guaranteed tastegasm.*"

I laugh, reading the note one more time, staring at the curves in her handwriting, the deliberate neatness of it. She writes like I bet she builds cabinets—determined, orderly, and organized, but with a little bit of flair and panache.

Flair? *Panache?*

What the bloody hell?

What am I now? A crime scene investigator? A handwriting analyst?

I blink the thoughts away, take the offending vegetables inside, and then serve them to Ethan at dinnertime.

He surveys them skeptically, but he's more daring with this food group than I am, so he takes a bite and murmurs, "These are strangely . . . sort of kind of good."

That is as big a seal of approval as one can get, especially coming from the tween.

I try them next, considering the flavors as I chew. They're subtle but tasty too.

Melt in my mouth? No.

But they are strangely sort of kind of good.

"You are correct," I say. "Shall I serve you these every night?"

"Hmm. Maybe not every night. Unless we can have dessert too."

"Brilliant idea. How about we bake brownies?"

His answer is a resounding yes.

After we finish dinner and clean up, we mix the batter, him dropping a dollop of the chocolate mixture onto my nose and me doing the same to him. Naturally, that requires a photo, so I snag my mobile, snap a shot, then send it to Aunt Jane.

Her reply is swift.

Aunt Jane: Send some of those brownies straightaway! Also, give that boy a kiss from me.

Liam: Brownies in the mail as we speak. Kisses commencing in 3, 2, 1 . . .

. . .

I set the phone down.

"Want to know the only thing better than baking brownies in August?" I ask Ethan.

"Sure. Tell me."

"Swimming while they cook."

"That's dope," he declares.

Once we put the batter in the oven, we're the dopest as we race each other out to the pool. He cannonballs, then splashes me as I jackknife in. "You're the rotten egg," he shouts.

"Obviously," I toss back loudly before I dive under and execute a shark attack that sends him into peals of laughter.

We take turns on the slide then devise a series of races, and the whole time I steal occasional glances at my neighbor's yard, hoping to catch a glimpse of her over the wooden fence between our homes.

Hoping she'll hear our shouts and splashes.

Hoping she might peer over the fence, wave, and say, "Can we join you?"

I'd say, "Yes, of course," and then we'd go for a dip.

That's appealing for so many reasons. Far too many reasons, like bikinis and droplets of water sliding down soft skin.

Because in my imaginary life, she'd wear a tiny bikini and Ethan would be in bed, and the guaranteed tastegasms would be of an entirely different variety.

*   *   *

The next morning, I return the clean Pyrex dish to her deck with some brownies in it and a note on the pan that says, *Good in the kitchen, as promised.*

Later that evening, I find a note under my door that reads: *Oh, so very good.*

This time when I study her penmanship, it seems neat but also a little more swoopy and seductive than before.

Perhaps I'm reading too much into green beans and brownies. Or perhaps I'm wanting the wrong things from the woman next door.

10

———

LIAM

It's tempting, I admit, to use the tagline "Good in bed" above my photo.

After all, that kind of slogan would entice me to click on someone's dating profile.

I didn't work on it the night I talked to January after my ride, but a few days later, I remove my sunglasses, setting them down on the sidewalk table where I'm indulging in an early evening drink with my sister, and I type those words into the profile I'm creating.

"What do you think?" I swivel my iPad to face my sister. Her son, Spencer, only a few years older than Ethan, is playing Frisbee in the town square with him as a squadron of ducks quack at them.

Kerri peers at the Boyfriend Material app on the screen, then recoils. "I don't want to hear about you being a good shag."

I roll my eyes. "That's not the point. The point is what do you think about it as a headline for a dating app?"

"Yes, that's still my answer, brother of mine," she says. "I don't want to think about your dating, your mating, your shagging, or your snogging."

I cover my heart with my hand, as if overcome. "Aw, you still think of me as your sweet little brother?"

She arches a brow. "I don't believe I've ever thought of you as sweet. Does anybody? Because you're not, actually."

I tut, shaking my head. "I'm very, very sweet."

"No. A pop tart is sweet. A steal of a deal on a bottle of wine is sweet. 'Sweet' is a word that literally no one has used to describe you. You are dry, droll, and sarcastic."

I shoot her a look. "That sounds exactly like you."

She preens, lifting her glass. "Takes one to know one."

"So, from one droll person to another, neither one of us is sweet?"

"That is true. But only one of us is trying to get on a dating app," she points out. Then her tone softens. "So tell me, what are you looking for in a woman?"

An image of my next-door neighbor sashays before my eyes.

Her lush brown hair.

Her inked arms.

Her pouty lips.

And most of all, her quick mouth and her agile wit.

But it's crazy to think of January in this context. Getting involved with the next-door neighbor is a recipe for trouble. Plus, she's already drawn her lines clearly. She's not interested in a man right now.

I soldier on, stopping to take a drink of my red wine. "Someone smart, funny, and kind, who loves animals and doesn't want to play the field."

"Don't forget—she needs to like cocky men who brag about their bedroom prowess."

"I still say it's a brilliant tagline, and since you're not the best person to give me advice on this subject, I'm going to ask someone who is," I say, then send a quick text to my friend Summer in New York City. She's been good mates with my cousin Oliver since they were thirteen, so I've come to know her too, and have relied on her for occasional advice about women.

Liam: Question. Should I use the headline "Good in Bed" for a dating profile? I feel like it's incredibly clear and totally direct.

She replies with several GIFs of a woman spitting out a drink of water. I show her replies to my sister. Kerri laughs and gestures to the screen. "See? Even your friend thinks it's a bad idea."

I study the GIFs then stab my finger against the screen for emphasis. "No, she's amused by it. That's what this says. She thinks I'm funny."

Kerri rolls her brown eyes. "I don't think she's amused by you. I think she finds *you* amusing. There's a difference."

Hmm. I think she's wrong.

Best to ask though.

. . .

Liam: My sister says that you're laughing at me rather than with me. I contend that your GIFs mean you think I'm a world-class humor producer.

Summer: I see you still suffer from the inability to read the nuance in front of your face.

Kerri lifts both brows approvingly when she reads the answer. "I like your friend. She knows exactly what you're like."

"I can read nuance just fine. All day long, I read mammals who can't speak."

My sister's eyes roll back into her head. "Oh, right. Being a vet means you're good at dating and good at understanding women because you're good at understanding pussycats and dogs. Your logic is so impeccable, Liam."

I square my shoulders. "Why, thank you very much."

"Oh, hi," says a new voice. "You must be the new guy." A blonde woman with a cheery grin has stopped by our table. "You're the gentleman who's just bought the yellow house on Mallard Lane, aren't you?"

I give her a smile. "Why, yes, I am."

"I'm Nina Clawson. I run the boba tea shop. I'd been hoping to run into you. Would you like to go on a date with my sister?"

Did she just say that?

I glance at Kerri, who rolls her eyes. I suppose that's a yes. Nina *did* just say that.

Since I'm new in town, and what is an app but a dating intermediary, I decide to treat this the same way I would check out someone's profile to learn more about her. "Why don't you tell me about your sister?"

The peppy blonde proceeds to rattle off the details—Maya is thirty-eight; loves Anna Kendrick movies, Kristin Hannah books, Adele's music; prefers coffee over tea, curry over Chinese; and am I free next weekend?

Damn.

That's speed matchmaking.

But before I can answer—and I'm not sure what I'd say—Nina swipes on her phone and shows me a photo.

Oh.

Oh, yes.

With a button nose and bow-shaped lips, her sister is quite cute.

I send a smug *I told you so* glance to Kerri, then agree to a date with Nina's sister. "That sounds fantastic."

Why not?

This is easier than an app.

Way easier.

I exchange numbers with Nina, and when she walks away, Kerri shoots death rays at me from her eyes. "What is wrong with the universe?"

"Seems like the universe knows a good thing when it sees it," I tease.

"I bet you walk into your backyard and money falls from a tree too."

"Well, I planted it first, but that sounds about right."

"It's ridiculous that you've been in town for barely a week and you've gotten a date from somebody literally passing you on the street."

I blow on my fingernails. "When you've got it, you've got it, apparently."

Ms. Right, here I come—the tastegasms and temptation of my neighbor be damned.

11

LIAM

On Monday morning, I finish my tea, set down the cup, then hold my arms out for inspection.

"So, what's the verdict? How do I look?"

Ethan scrunches up the corner of his lips, then washes his cereal bowl as he gives me the most cursory of cursory appraisals. "Like a dad."

I roll my eyes. "Seriously?"

Turning off the tap, he nods. "Seriously. You seriously look like a dad."

I gesture grandly to my outfit. "I am wearing scrubs. How is that a dad outfit?"

He shrugs. "You look like a dad to me. You are a dad. Why is it so bad if you look like one?"

"I'm not wearing white sneakers. Didn't you say you'd disown me if I did?" I wave at my sneakers, which are definitely not white. They are, in fact, Vans. "Summer approved these, which means they are cool."

"Fine. Your scrubs and your Vans are"—he stops to sketch air quotes—"*cool.*" He says it as if the word tastes bitter. "But you need to stop with the lingo. You just can't do it. It sounds so wrong coming out of your mouth."

I park my hands on my hips. "Maybe you just need to admit that you can't handle my coolness."

"Dad, it's not even *cool* anymore. We don't say *cool*. We say *clean*. Okay?"

What in the bloody hell kind of nonsense is that? "Clean? My outfit is clean? As in neat and tidy, or as in not on drugs?"

"No," he says, choking on a laugh. "Clean means nice, excellent, tight."

"So my outfit is clean?"

"Your outfit is clean as in neat and tidy. But it is not clean as in nice, excellent, tight."

I hold up my arms in surrender. "I'm done."

"Good plan, Dad. Very good plan."

We make our way to the door, Ethan stopping to grab his baseball mitt from the table—the one that will vamoose when the new furniture arrives soon. I picture January assembling it. Then I picture how much I'll enjoy watching her assemble it. Then I tell myself to stop enjoying the images so much.

I unlock the front door. "Do you have everything? Did you put on sunscreen?"

"I did. I also just had an idea. If I tell you you're cool, will you play baseball with me after work?" He sounds devilishly strategic, and I'm impressed. I love a Machiavellian brain, especially in a nearly ten-year-old.

I stroke my chin, pretending to consider it. "All right. If you insist."

"You're cool," he says, with a couple of *I got you* nods.

I open the door, let him go ahead of me, then pull it closed and lock it. "Joke's on you. I was going to play baseball with you anyway."

He shrugs and gives me a smile. "I know. I just like to pretend I actually think you're cool."

I ruffle his hair as we go down the steps. "You are proof sarcasm is genetic."

"I am."

As he bounds ahead of me, I linger on that word— *genetic*. Like that, my mind makes the familiar trip back to Florida and his early years. How else did genetics show up back then? When he walked? When he talked?

What was his first word?

Shit.

I never asked his mom.

Now I'll never know. I'll never know, either, how he looked toddling around the house, flinging mashed peas from a high chair, or learning to ride a bike.

I'll never know what it's like to have comforted him when he tumbled and got that first scraped knee. He could already wheel around fine on his own when he arrived in New York.

I blink the longing away.

Focus on the here and now.

Once inside the garage, we grab our gleaming new bikes from the rack. I roll them out to the driveway, stopping to press the button to close the garage behind us. As I strap on my helmet, my eyes are drawn to next door where—just my luck—January is loading a toolbox into her truck.

I devour the view. She's wearing work boots, jeans, and a tight pink T-shirt with a logo reading "Jackie of All Trades." And hell, does her arse look great in those jeans. But then, it looks great in everything. Probably in nothing too, come to think of it.

I banish the dirty thought as she swivels around, raises her shades, then says, "Are you off for a bike ride?"

It comes out sounding confused, even though we're both standing here with bikes. "Are we?"

"You're in scrubs," she says, pointing. "That's why I asked."

"I look pretty cool in scrubs, don't I?"

She arches a doubtful brow. "I think if they had pink unicorns on them, they'd be cooler."

"Duly noted."

"And where are you heading, Ethan?" she asks him.

But before he can answer, I chime in, unable to resist poking fun at my kid. "Is it your papier-mâché camp? Oh, wait, is it pottery making? No, it's underwater basket weaving, right?"

He cracks up then turns to January and squeaks, "Baseball camp! I like baseball. Actually, that's wrong. I love baseball."

"You have excellent taste in sports," she says.

"He's a junkie for America's pastime," I tell her. "As am I."

Is that genetic too? Or did it start when he moved in with me? Certainly, his love of the sport grew stronger. Regular attendance at Yankee Stadium will do that to a lad.

Ethan smacks his palm against his forehead. "Dad, I did forget my sunscreen." He sets the bike on the driveway, races up the steps, and unlocks the door.

While he's inside, January cuts across the lawn, standing near me in the driveway. "So you're going to ride into work looking like that?"

My brow furrows. "Yes. Is that a problem?"

"You realize you'll get double the number of dates that you did sitting at the wine bar the other day."

Gossip had carried the tale to her long before I had a chance to share the story.

"Double? More than when I dine outside? Whoa."

"Hello? Hot, healthy, eco-conscious vet who rides a bike to work?"

I like the sound of that when she says it. My skin sizzles. "So, I'm a hot vet?"

She rolls her eyes, then shoos me away. "Don't act like you didn't know that, Liam." She flicks her fingers, telling me to be on my way, as Ethan returns and hops onto his bike. I hop onto mine, waving goodbye, and I savor that very lovely compliment that I shouldn't like so much, but I do.

Oh, I absolutely do.

* * *

After I drop Ethan off at the baseball park, I ride a few miles to the building marked with a sign that reads: LUCKY FALLS VETERINARY PRACTICE, DR. HARRIS, DVM. The practice is on a side street also occupied by a spa and a hair salon. You can get pampered while your pet gets poked. It's only a couple of miles away from Duck Falls.

I pull into the lot, my eyes drifting to the sign, my heart squeezing tightly as I think about *that* Dr. Harris. The first one. The reason I moved from one coast to the other.

That Dr. Harris waits for me in the small parking lot, next to my mum, who leans against the hood of her car, holding his hand. I rest the bike against the side of the building, then head over to them.

"Hi, Mum. Hi, Dad."

"Hi, Liam," he says in that gruff voice I've known my entire life, the sound that I heard booming up the stairs when I was in trouble, the sound that I heard shouting *Yes!* when I won science awards.

The voice has varied. That gruffness was tempered with sweetness after my first broken heart, and again after I first learned the shocking news that I had a son, when he told me that he would help me figure out how to be a great dad.

All of those memories collide at once, and they pummel me with an unexpected wave of emotion. I should be used to those overwhelming feelings when I'm around him these days.

I swallow them down, shove them out of sight, and put on my best chipper face as I join them. He squints at me from behind his glasses, and I hide a wince.

"How's it going, Liam? Are you ready for today?" He's all tough and serious. He's softer with animals, but with his kids, he's always kept the pedal on the stoic side.

"I am, Dad. Just remind me—is the tailbone still connected to the leg bone?"

He laughs and claps me on the shoulder, his palm wrapping around me. "Good one. It's the caudal vertebrae."

My mouth forms an exaggerated O. "Is that what it's called? I had no idea."

He shakes his head. "Smart-ass. Anyway, I wanted to bring you this." He turns around and peers into the car, searching for a few more seconds than usual.

"On the console, love," my mum says. He reaches inside, grabs a thermos of English breakfast tea—unless I very much miss my guess—then gives it to me.

Just like my mum gave him every day before work, the tradition now handed down from father to son.

A lump forms in my throat at the way he's trying to make this seem like a normal transition. As if all he's done is retire and hand over his beloved practice to me.

I take the thermos, trying to keep my tone even, so it's not as wobbly as I feel. "Thank you."

He gives me an almost imperceptible nod, then tips his forehead toward the light-blue cottage-style building that houses the veterinary practice that he ran for more than twenty years. "I appreciate you doing this."

He's not big on hearts and flowers, so his spoken gratitude is the equivalent of a brass band marching through town in my honor.

"And I appreciate you giving me the chance to help out," I say, though that hardly seems sufficient. Or accurate—"giving me the chance" implies that he had a choice, that to continue was an option.

It took him long enough to accept the facts and step down. My mum practically begged him.

A few months ago, when he rang me up, potholes in his voice, and asked if I would come home and take over, I didn't think twice. I simply said yes. I had five business partners at my practice in New York. I was also the junior vet. He ran this practice solo.

Now he stares at the front door, shiny with its fresh coat of white paint. It's something Mum took care of—hiring painters to spruce up the place. New paint for the new vet.

"Are you ready for next month?" I ask, trying to focus on practical matters—in this case, his third surgery coming up.

He scoffs and waves a hand. "Don't worry about me."

"But I do."

"We all do," my mum chimes in.

"I'm going to be fine, so let me worry about you." He takes a few steps toward the door. "Do you have everything you need in there?"

He rattles off all the standard supplies of any veterinary practice, and I simply nod, letting him know that I'm all sorted. At the door, he barrels inside, doing his damnedest to show me around, even though I've spent the last week prepping and familiarizing myself with the clinic.

Getting ready to take over his business as my father goes blind.

* * *

Twenty minutes later, the vet tech comes in—a pink-haired fifty-something woman with triple ear piercings and a sweet cooing voice that all the dogs seem to love —and we get to work.

The hardest part is when the clients start asking, "Is everything okay with your dad?"

I do my best. Give them a smile and the scripted line. "He just thought it was time. He's ready for a change. Ready to retire. Now, let's take a look at Purr-cutio's teeth."

My dad doesn't want to share the true reason, not wanting anyone to feel sorry for him. I'm not going to be the one to say, "Oh, well, it turns out he has this rare disease where he's going blind, and he's going to require five surgeries and still lose most of his vision."

Besides, the story is plausible. He's sixty-two, near retirement age. Even though the truth is that he would have worked for as long as he possibly could have.

At the end of the day, my final client arrives, a gray-haired woman with sharp blue eyes and a Papillon-Chihuahua mix.

"She's so picky. She only likes to eat the steak or chicken or turkey I prepare for her."

"Rather than dog kibble?"

"Yes. She turns up her nose at it when they feed her at the doggie bed-and-breakfast when I go to see my friends in the city overnight."

"And how long have you been feeding her home-cooked meals?"

"About a year now."

"Perhaps ask the B&B if they have a fridge. Bring her what she's used to."

"Brilliant," she says, as if I just answered all her woes. Then she swings the conversation in a sharp right turn. "On to other matters, Dr. Harris. I live down the street from you in Duck Falls. What are the chances you'd like to take my daughter Missy out for dinner?"

Huh. Seems January was wrong.

I didn't need to ride my bike to attract another date.

But all things considered, this seems much better than a dating app.

It's a dating app delivered to my doorstep.

Like Grubhub for women.

* * *

Later, when Ethan is taking a shower, I pop outside to check the mailbox, since I forgot to when I returned home. And, lucky me, January is kneeling in her front yard, tending to the flowers.

Her gaze catches mine. "How was your first day, Doctor Dolittle? Did any of your clients try to set you up? Or was it all of them? My money is on the latter."

Laughing, I head over and join her. "I only had two requests for dates."

"I'd have expected four. You're losing your touch." She brushes her hands against her legs and leaves streaks of soil on them. As she rises, she pushes her hair out of her eyes. The whole effect is wildly sexy. I never knew I was that into her type. That is, if she is a type. If she is, I would call it "insanely self-sufficiently sexy."

"I have to content myself with two, or three," I say, continuing the conversation.

She pats me on the arm. "This town—I don't know if you've noticed, but it's a small town where men are in short supply. Who's the next date with?"

"A woman named Missy. Betty Juniper's daughter."

January's eyes light up. "Oh, Missy's great. Outgoing and friendly. She owns the lingerie shop and does such a bang-up job that she's nabbed 'Best of' accolades in all the area newspapers and lists. She's open-minded about nearly everything except fish."

"Fish? Why's that?"

"In high school, she threw up fish sticks one day, and everyone called her Fishy Missy for days, and it really caused a lot of trauma for her. So don't order fish when you're with her."

"Good to know," I say, taking in this bizarre but important fact. "Perhaps I should come to you before every date and get a full briefing."

She smiles. "That's not a bad idea. Think of me as your dating insider."

I like the idea of spending more time with her. I hate the constant reminders that she's not the one I'm dating.

But that's fine.

It's perfectly, absolutely fine.

At least, that's what I'm telling myself.

12

LIAM

It's Thursday night, date night.

Ethan's at Kerri's house, and I have the place to myself to get ready. I shower, get dressed, and check the time. About thirty minutes before I meet Nina's sister Maya at the wine bar. Just enough time to walk to town. Why drive when I have feet or a pair of bicycle tires?

I head down the front steps as the familiar rumble of a pink truck echoes across the lawn, pulling into the driveway next door. Like I'm Pavlov's dog, a rush of heat slides down my spine at the sound, then spreads across my chest when I see January cut the engine. A grin tugs at my lips. This is my favorite time of day—any time I run into her.

She opens the door and steps out of the truck, her daughter swinging open the door on the other side, barely giving anyone a second glance as she rushes up the steps, propelled by jet fuel, the front door slamming behind her in a dark-blonde spitfire blur.

"Everything okay?"

January waves a hand toward the cheetah of a teenager. "Oh, she's totally fine. She has a FaceTime sesh with her friend Audrey and can't be late. They're deciding what to sample in their next YouTube video—panda cookies or chocolate mushrooms."

"Not panda cookies, please."

"It's a brand. Not made of pandas. Or for pandas."

I wipe a hand across my brow. "Whew. I feel loads better."

January eyes me up and down, bright blue eyes traveling along my frame. "I see you're in your dating gear."

"I am indeed." I tug at an imaginary bow tie. "I couldn't decide between the bow tie or the stonewashed jeans, so I wore *this* instead. Good compromise?"

With that deadpan expression I enjoy so much, she nods. "Yes, but I would give good money to see you in stonewashed denim."

I gesture to my house. "How much? Twenty bucks?"

"Bargain basement. Do it," she says with a sly grin.

"Don't tempt me. Twenty bucks covers wine."

She arches one dubious brow. "You clearly haven't set foot in Oscar's Wine Bar, then."

"True. Kerri did pay the other day. I'll take ten, then. Enough for a tip. Should I go put them on right now?"

"Do it, do it," she chants.

I tip my head toward the street, laughing. "Next time, I promise to give you a fashion show, but I should be getting on." I take a beat, studying her and wondering if her gaze isn't tinged with perhaps a touch of longing. Or maybe I'm simply wishing. "Unless you'd like to join me for a walk into town . . ."

I leave that invitation hanging in the air as my chest flips with the hope that she'll say yes. It's strange, this sensation of waiting for something, wanting something.

Her smile spreads slow and easy, and her *yes* seems to float across her eyes.

But I don't want to assume.

"I would love to." It's not dry, it's not sarcastic, and it's not deadpan.

They're just four lovely words that I relish hearing from her.

She holds up her hands. "Just give me a second to wash up. I was working all day. And to let Wednesday know she's cooking for me tonight."

"She cooks?"

January lights up with a cartoonishly large smile. "Yes! I highly recommend acquiring children who are useful. She loves to cook. I think it's because she loves workarounds and she searches for cooking hacks for nearly every recipe."

"Because recipes shouldn't be followed?"

"Psh. Hacks are so much more fun."

"I suppose I can't argue with that."

She darts inside and returns a minute later, showing off her clean palms. "My hands are spick-and-span, and my kid is going to make pasta salad with zucchini noodles instead of noodle noodles. Feel free to shudder."

I do. "Zucchini is the worst."

She pats my shoulder. "You don't know what you're missing, doc. I bet I could get you to like veggies. You did enjoy the green beans, didn't you?"

"They were decent," I grumble.

"Aww. See? The veggie lifestyle is growing on you. Wednesday and I make the most awesome salads in Northern California. My mom is a convert. She used to be all carbs and meat, and now she's becoming a salad lover. I'm working on you next, neighbor."

The way she says *neighbor* sends a wicked thrill through me. Maybe because she delivers it with a twinkle in her blue eyes, with a saucy lift of her lips. Like it's the start of something.

Maybe I should say yes to her mutant pasta dish. Maybe I do want to try zucchini noodles. But I can't quite let on how much yet, so I say, "I dunno. Zucchini noodles seem like noodles gone wrong."

"They are noodles gone right. I promise."

There's an invitation somewhere in there, and I want to RSVP to it, but instead I just nod toward town. "Shall we?"

"Let's go." As we set off, she adds, "Now, Liam, am I the pillow tonight?"

I give her a blank look, but quickly dig into my bag of at-the-ready replies. "You'd like me to sleep on you?"

"You are so good with innuendos. And with blatantly bringing up sex," she says, shaking her head in amusement.

"True, true. One of my many skills is the ability to weave sex into many conversations."

As we turn the corner, she makes a rolling gesture with her hands. "Work with me. Remember, pillows as a lubricant? A lubricant to sleep? So you're going to use me as lube before your date?"

I laugh, getting it this time. "Who's saucy now? I'm pretty sure you just went full innuendo."

She gives me a *you got me* shrug. "Maybe I did."

I raise a too-suave-for-words eyebrow. "For what it's worth, I think you'd make fantastic lube, January."

We both laugh, and perhaps that means she's enjoying the naughty edge to the conversation too.

But it's time to downshift, since I do have a date, and I shouldn't show up with other women on my mind. That's ungentlemanly, not to mention unfair to Maya.

I steer us to safer ground. "Did you have a busy day?"

"Exhausting. I built a new door for a family room after a teenage son swung on it too many times and it came unhinged."

"Boys can be part monkey. Is the work done?"

"One more day. It's looking good, and it's a gig I busted my butt to land. They decided to start over from scratch. New framing, new paint, matching wood, and so on. I was competing against Big Beams Construction, and I wasn't sure I was going to land it. They're a national chain."

"I've heard the ads. They're constantly trying to undercut local carpenters, aren't they?"

She heaves a frustrated sigh. "Absolutely. I had to lower my bid a little bit because I really wanted the gig. It can be disheartening, constantly feeling like you're looking behind you, watching for how they're going to try and cut you off at the knees. But hey, that's competition. You just have to keep up with it," she says, finishing on a chin-up note. That seems to be her MO—finding the positive, looking ahead.

"How did you get into the business?"

"My dad is a carpenter. But I always loved making things. I was the one in the house who assembled desks from Target or Walmart. I put together an elliptical machine my mom ordered when she went on her cardio kick when I was fourteen."

I shoot her an approving look. "An elliptical at age fourteen? Very impressive."

"What's most impressive is my mom still uses it. Two decades later," she says, shimmying her shoulders.

I blink, exaggerating shock. "Okay, that is one helluva machine." Then, I correct myself. "I mean, that is one helluva job you did putting it together."

She flashes me a bright, pleased grin. "Thank you. And to tell you the truth, I'm extra proud of its long life because my mom is the queen worrier. She has earned all the worry badges any mom can ever earn, along with stripes, tassels, and epaulets. She was convinced it was going to break every time she used it. She'd call me out to the garage constantly to make sure it was safe to use. Finally, after a year of her machine working perfectly, she stopped worrying."

"So basically, your assembly skills are top-notch?"

She gives a sashay of her hips. There's a gleam in her eyes too. She's proud of her abilities, and that's wildly appealing. "Your words, Liam."

"I guess we'll have to see how top-notch they are, though, when IKEA finally shows up. Then I'll be the judge," I say with mock intensity.

"Put me to the test, Liam. I can't wait to show off my skills to you."

She has no idea how many tests I want to put her through, how many skills I'd love to show her, starting with how well I can brush my lips across her neck, down her throat, between her breasts . . . but I sweep those thoughts into the dirty-thought closet and shut the door, locking them up with the rest. "So, you've always been handy, it sounds like. And then you put that to use in your business?"

"Yes, but in my dad's business first. When I started working with him, I learned the tricks of the trade. And my mother makes soap that she sells at local markets, so we're all handy in different ways. It's a family thing, I suppose."

"Same here," I say. "Taking over the vet practice from Dr. Harris Senior and all." I don't go into the details, because I don't want to feel sad right now, so I segue back to her. "Do you have any siblings? Actually, how do I not know this yet? I can't believe I've lived here for two weeks and I haven't asked you this." I smile, but I'm genuinely surprised, since we've talked about so much already.

She nudges me with her elbow. "I'm actually a little disappointed too, Liam. I have been marking off the days, wondering when you were ever going to ask me if I have siblings."

"And fourteen days later, I finally did. So, siblings?"

"I have a sister. She lives in San Francisco."

"And what is her name? Is it Leap Year?"

She laughs, and it's such a lovely sound that I think I could become addicted to it. "Yes, that's her."

As the twinkling lights from the town square grow bigger and brighter, I ask, "What is her name for real?"

"You're not going to believe it."

"Actually, I bet I will."

"It's April."

"Then you need a July and an October, and you've got the start of all the fiscal quarters accounted for."

"Exactly. And you have a sister too?"

"Kerri's in town. My other sister, Toni, is thirty minutes away. Kerri has two kids, and so does Toni."

"And is that the required number for Harris children?"

"Seems to be. I guess I didn't get the memo." I flick my gaze her way, waiting for a response but not sure what I want her to say. Why should she say anything? We already had the kid conversation at IKEA. There isn't much more to discuss.

And talking about kids reminds me that we aren't entirely on the same page.

Entirely.

That's a lie.

We aren't remotely on the same page.

When we near the wine bar, I take a beat, draw a deep breath, then say, "Okay, so as my dating insider, what do I need to know about Maya?"

"Ah, I have the dirt for you," she says in a conspiratorial whisper. "She's chatty. Likes to talk. But she's funny."

"Funny is good. I like funny."

"Sweet lady. Not full of herself at all. She works at the glitter factory."

"Nothing wrong with glitter."

"Glitter is awesome. I love glitter," she says.

"You seem like a glitter person."

"Why's that?"

"Because you like pink," I answer.

"Pink and glitter go hand in hand?"

"Like dogs and loyalty. Like cats and disdain."

"Fine," she says with a grumble. "I like glitter and pink and hammers and blueprints."

I try to hide a grin, enjoying all the sides of her. "Yes, you do."

"And one more thing about Maya. She's a cat person. She has a big orange boy cat named Saul," January adds as we near the town square.

"Good to know. I can ask to see pictures of him."

January's mouth forms an O. Her nose crinkles.

"Wait. I shouldn't ask to see cat photos?"

January winces. "Yeah . . . I should have led with this. You probably won't have to ask for photos." The words come out like an apology.

"Because she'll show them to me of her own accord?"

Another wince. Another contrite smile. "She'll bring the cat."

Blinking, I shake my head. That can't be possible. But then, maybe it can. "She's bringing a cat on the date? Is it a therapy cat?"

"No. Well, it's more like she's therapy for the cat."

"I'm not sure I'm following."

"The cat can't be left alone, so she brings the cat everywhere."

I stare at her, bug-eyed, then set a hand on her shoulder. "You're my dating insider. That's information I should have known a few days ago."

She cringes, *I'm sorry* written all over her face. "I should have told you. I literally just remembered. I think I might've been trying to block it out of my mind."

"Yeah. I'd block that out too, but I feel like I'm not going to be able to," I say as a plaintive meow comes from outside Oscar's Wine Bar.

Sounds more like a warning bell, an ill omen for my foray into romancing with felines.

Only I wish this walk was the start of a different date.

A date that can't be.

Because I'd rather be having zucchini noodles right now.

13

LIAM

I barely get a word in edgewise.

The second I walk up near the wine bar and spot the cute brunette with the popsicle-blue glasses, she smiles, waves, and says, "Nina warned me."

"About what?" I ask, taken aback as I grab the seat across from her.

She waggles long fingernails painted with cherry-red stripes. "She told me the new guy in town was honey on a stick, sugar on a stick, a chocolate-covered banana on a stick."

"Banana?" I file away a mental note to ask January if that's a good thing.

Maya waves a hand, dismissing that. She points at me, sizing me up. "Nope. That's wrong. You're a swirly lollipop. And Nina did not properly warn me about that. Oh sure, she warned me that you're British, and therefore charming. But that's understandable, because a woman needs to be warned that she'll melt on cue with that kind of accent."

But I've barely spoken, I want to say. Instead, I smile and answer with "Reasonable warning indeed. Generally, my countrymen like to give women a heads-up so our accents don't cause an overabundance of swooning." Might as well try to live up to the charming part, at least. I nod to the creature in her lap, then scratch his head. The big orange guy lifts his face and stares at me, asking for more. "You must be Maya, and I hear this is your friend, Saul."

"My friend Saul—please. More like my ball and chain," she scoffs as I pet his head a little longer. "But yes, I'm Maya, and this cat is my albatross. But it's nice to meet you, doctor, and I bet any minute Saul will cast a disdainful glare in your direction, because he is a mercurial male cat."

"Cats can be mercurial," I say with a smile. I stroke between his ears. "Particularly male cats. Isn't that right, Saul?"

Her brown eyes pop as I talk to the cat. She cocks her head like she's listening to him. "Doc," she whispers, *eureka*-style. "He's purring. The devil purrs for no one. The devil doesn't even purr for me. What is it with this creature?" She slides a hand down his back. "Maybe that's his way of saying he needed this all along? A moment with a hot British vet at a wine bar. Get in line, pussycat. I want my moment too, dammit."

I'm not entirely sure that we're going to have a moment, but Maya is sort of adorable in a manic kind of way.

She also doesn't seem to need much conversational

effort from me, since she's keeping up the chatter for both of us.

"But I can't get a break from this cat, who insists on sitting on my lap all the time," she says, her eyes plaintive, full of worry. I set my hands in my lap as she continues, "If I take him off my lap, he jumps back on. He rubs up against me. He follows me from room to room. And all I want is to spend time with this man who is asking how Saul is and stroking the devil's chin."

I'm not sure if she's speaking to me about the devil or to the devil about me.

"You're the neediest male known to malekind," she says.

Yup, she's still talking to Saul, and I'm not entirely sure I'm needed here. She might very well be a self-sustaining date.

She waggles a finger at the ginger creature. "But I have a date with a vet. And I am going to get answers. Take that, cat," she says, sassy as a reality TV star.

Or perhaps I am needed.

Just for something other than my company.

For my expertise.

"Would you like to order, Maya?" I suggest, since I'm pretty sure I need a glass or four right now for this unexpected vet therapy session.

And something to soak it up.

Once we order white wine and a plate of cheese and olives for an appetizer, she lets out a long, needy sigh, like a balloon losing all its air. "I can't mince words anymore," she says.

"I didn't think you were."

"I'll beg for help if I have to. Dr. Harris, I'm going to level with you."

"Please do," I say, patiently waiting.

She flaps her hands at the big orange tabby in her lap. "Why won't he leave my side?" Her voice threatens to break, and my heart softens more.

Perhaps this is why Maya needed this date. To deal with her feline homunculus. "Tell me more about him."

She does. She spills all, the whole tale of her cat, finishing with "You're wonderful. You listened. You listened to every word." She sounds as if that's never happened before. "My last vet didn't listen at all. I was seeing a vet in the city."

"I have some thoughts on what might be going on with Saul," I say.

We chat about options for clingy cats with possessive behavior, until she slumps happily in her chair, a smile spreading across her face, bliss in her features as she announces, "This is the best date I have ever been on in my life because you're smart, kind, and patient, and I just got an hour of free veterinary care and cat therapy."

Her hand flies to her mouth, then she removes it. "Shoot. I'm sorry. I don't want you to think I was using you. I really like you, Dr. Harris. A lot. I like you a lot, and you're handsome and smart and English, and I wouldn't mind seeing you again and hearing you again and listening to your charming voice talk about cats. Do you want to go out again? We could go for a walk—the three of us maybe. I could put him in his harness. He's great on a leash."

I shake my head, giving her a soft smile. "If you need any more help with Saul, why don't you set up a time and come see me at the office, and we can sort through some of these issues? I had a lovely time tonight, but I think perhaps we're better off as vet and client."

I pay the bill, walk her out, and wish her well, feeling oddly glad it didn't work out.

* * *

"On a scale of one to ten, was it the weirdest date ever?"

The question comes from Oliver on the other end of the phone as I walk through the town square, post cat-date.

I laugh, shaking my head. "No. God, no. The weirdest one I've ever been on was the ad exec who couldn't stop picking her teeth with her fork to get the barbecue out of them, and she covered her mouth with her hand as if I couldn't see her. She did it all throughout the meal."

"Why did you just remind me? I tried to block that from my mind."

"You literally just asked, wanker."

"Yes, but you should protect me from horror stories. You know I don't like them."

"Because you have your own horror stories."

"Indeed. Like Hazel, who stalked my apartment six days in a row after we broke up. Just . . . lying in ambush. I had to call Summer to help me escape from her, to pretend to be my girlfriend."

I laugh. "And I'm sure that pained you, to have to play make-believe with Summer. How devastating to spend extra time with a woman who you're secretly wildly attracted to."

"Whoever said I'm secretly wildly attracted to her?"

"I actually just did." I wander past the ice cream shop, the sweet scent of waffle cones drifting out the doorway and giving me an idea. "I need to nip off. I'll text you in a minute. I'm popping into the ice cream shop."

I say goodbye, head inside, survey the menu, then order a pint of Chocolate Peanut Butter Dream, which sounds like the perfect end to an imperfect first date in Duck Falls.

When the hazel-eyed woman with the toned arms who runs the shop hands me the pint, she slides me a business card along with it. "I'm Valeria Rodriquez. I've heard about you. Give me a call sometime. I'll make you your own flavor." She adds a wink, even though I heard the wink in her words loud and clear.

And I don't mind her directness. Don't mind it at all.

"Thanks." I tuck the card into my back pocket. "A special flavor sounds brilliant."

I don't feel a spark with Valeria, but maybe I will on a date. Maybe that's when sparks happen. Not when you first meet, right?

On the way home, a text from Oliver flashes at me.

Oliver: Cat lady is a definite no, then?

Liam: Cat aside, free vet consult aside, and drama aside, I didn't feel a spark.

Oliver: A spark matters.

Liam: Absolutely. It matters tons.

Oliver: What about the lady next door? Octoberfest? Fourth of July? Sunday Funday?

The back of my neck pricks. Is it that obvious? I don't even think I've told him much about January.

Liam: Her name is January, you twat. And what about her?

Oliver: You said she was going to assemble your furniture.

Liam: And you think that means there's a spark?

Oliver: I think it means there's a fox next door to you who wants to put together your coffee table, and I'm assuming the next thing you'll do is test the strength of it with her.

Liam: I appreciate you plotting out my sex life. Do you want to send step-by-step instructions next?

Oliver: I just ordered a guidebook for you. Amazon Prime. Coming in a few days.

Liam: Better yet, I'll just get the audiobook and start listening tonight.

A few seconds later, an email lands on my phone saying that the IKEA delivery will arrive next week.

Is it normal for an email from a big-box store to turn me on?

It is now because this email means January is coming over to assemble furniture. And that—that just gets me going.

Then again, *she* gets me going.

When I reach my street, I can't wait to give her the update on my couch, table, and chair. And telling her is going to be incredibly easy—she's on her porch sitting in her porch swing, her feet curled up under her, an e-reader in one hand, a glass of wine in the other, and a smile on her face as she chuckles at whatever's on the screen.

She takes a sip of her wine, looking fresh-faced and lovely in the moonlight.

When she glances over the top of the e-reader and catches sight of me, I don't even bother asking if she wants company. I turn into her yard, head up the steps, hold out the ice cream, and say, "Would you like some?"

I bought the pint hoping for this kind of kismet.

This kind of connection.

"I would love some."

Everything sparks as I sit next to her, and that's the trouble. But tonight, I'm going to invite trouble in.

14

JANUARY

As Liam sits next to me on my porch swing, I'm holding my breath, crossing my fingers, and offering prayers to the universe that he's endured a terrible date. Which probably makes me a horrible person, but still, I'm hunting for evidence.

I want a furrow in his brow, a beleaguered sigh like he can't believe that dates could be as bad as this date was tonight.

But I see none of that, so I steel myself for the opposite. For Exhibit A that perhaps he had a magnificent time.

Is there a hickey on his neck?

I peer as surreptitiously as I can, but I don't find a single black-and-blue splotch. Nor is his hair messed up as if fingers were run through it. His lips don't look ruddy or over-kissed.

I don't find any proof of a great time, even in the moonlight.

This should be reassuring, but it's not. The trouble

is, Liam looks the same as he did before he left. Maybe happier—is that the telltale sign that he had a great date?

He's grinning wildly.

I swallow the little spoonful of jealousy that's swirling in my mouth. I try to stomach the bitter taste of envy as I untuck my legs, straighten my spine, and point to the ice cream pint.

"Do you need a spoon?" I ask, a little too evenly, as I focus on practical matters.

He raises the pint, then says, "No. I thought I would just lick it straight from the container."

I roll my eyes. "Smart-ass."

I head inside, listening toward Wednesday's room. She's tapping away on her computer, probably still working on a website design. I pop into the kitchen, grab two spoons and some napkins, then return to the porch, the warmth of late summer wrapping around me, hugging me as I sit next to my handsome British neighbor, the good guy next door who is looking for Ms. Right.

Not me, not me, not me.

I swallow, bracing myself for the report he's about to give his dating insider. For the words that will go with the smile on his face.

"So . . . what's the verdict?" I ask as he digs into the ice cream and moans around it in culinary delight.

"Amazing. That's my verdict." He's pointing to the dessert.

I swat his leg before I realize we're not on swatting terms yet. Especially at this dark, quiet hour as crickets chirp, the silence of the small-town evening enrobing us.

His eyes lock with mine, and his voice is thoughtful as he asks, "Do you ever think about how hard it is to meet someone you truly connect with?"

In a heartbeat, the tension in me unwinds and floats away, rising to the sky, turning into stardust.

So it wasn't a great date.

That makes me ridiculously happy, even though it shouldn't make me feel anything at all.

He takes another spoonful of the ice cream, and I do the same, our utensils clinking inside the pint.

"So the date wasn't great?"

He shrugs. "It was fine. She's interesting and lively, though there's no need for a second. But I realized it's hard to click on a lot of levels." His eyes find mine, like he's eager for my opinion as he asks, "Don't you think?"

Chocolate melts on my tongue as I turn the question over in my mind. "I suppose that's true."

"It should be easier. There are, what, eight billion people on this planet? But still, what are the chances that you'll run into the right person for you?"

"The person you get along with."

"Someone you laugh with," he adds.

"Someone you respect." It's like we're finishing each other's sentences.

"And support." He digs the spoon in again and takes a bite, the metal sliding past his lips.

"Someone you want to kiss," I say, trying to mask my wondering about how his lips might taste right now. A little cold, a lot sweet.

All delicious.

"Someone you want to sleep with," he adds, and maybe he's not masking his thoughts either. Our gazes seem to linger for dizzying seconds—seconds that thrum through my veins. But then he returns to philosophical mode, holding an arm out wide and sighing. "And just like that, the choice gets narrower and narrower."

"And even narrower still," I add, following the contemplative direction of this conversation as I scoop another bite of the decadent ice cream. "Because you also have to meet the right person in the right place at the right time. Who wants the same things you do."

"That's the hardest part of all, isn't it?" His eyes align with mine, and my stomach jumps. It flips. It handsprings.

His brown eyes are intense, and it feels like a whole new level of eye contact that we're engaging in after his date that clearly went belly-up. He's not giving me sex eyes. There's something more in them. A connection perhaps.

"And that's how nearly eight billion funnels down to maybe, just maybe, one. If you're lucky," I say, a little melancholy.

He takes a beat and sets the spoon down on the swing. "Did you want the same things as Vince?"

I shake my head. "I don't think so. But I also don't think we had a chance to figure that out once we had a kid. Before then, yes. In college we wanted to have fun, to party, to have sex, to study a little bit, and to have a good time."

"Sounds like college," he says dryly. "Or so I'm told."

"You didn't go to any parties in college?"

He pats his chest. "Geek here. I didn't get invited."

I nudge him with my elbow, probably something else I shouldn't do. "You don't have to get invited. You just go."

"Gee, thanks for the tip. That's super helpful now."

I laugh then dive deeper into his question about Vince. "I suppose we were compatible at the time in other ways. We were career-oriented. I had this vision that once I graduated, I was going to be the CEO of a business or something. I don't even know what I wanted the business to be, but I thought I would be some badass chick running a consulting company. Funny thing is, I didn't even really know what consulting was—I just imagined that was what I would do. Then Wednesday came along, and that changed everything."

He arches a brow in a question. "It changed what you wanted to do with your life?"

I draw a deep breath. "I think so." I feel vulnerable admitting this, but also comfortable saying it to him. Liam makes me feel safe, like it's okay to open up, like he doesn't judge. He doesn't drift off during conversations like Vince did—he was barely there at times. "I wanted to raise her. I wanted that more than anything, and Vince made it possible. He wound up getting a job as a project manager at a tech company, and he did well enough so I could be home with her," I say, memories of those early years flashing before me. "He liked to play golf with his buddies on the weekend and hang out with the guys, and I wanted to raise my little girl and go to mommy groups, and I did that. I loved it, and I'm glad I did. I'm glad I had the chance, even though it was exhausting."

His smile is so soft, so genuine that it hooks into me, tugs at my heart. "You guys get along so great, you and Wednesday. All worth it, right?"

"One hundred percent. And I didn't even know that was what I wanted when I was pregnant. Until they put her in my arms, I didn't realize that I wanted to spend all my time with her," I say, and Liam's beaming, like he finds this the most delightful thing. My God, it's such an endearing look, but such a terrifying one too. It's a reminder that he wants more of that—having a baby in your arms—and I want none of it.

I try to laugh it off. "What? Why are you looking at me like that?"

He shrugs a little sheepishly. "I think that's lovely. It's great that you felt that way. That you knew what you wanted to do. That you did it."

"It was the only thing I felt certain about then, Liam." I lean a little closer, lowering my voice a bit more, compelled to share this with him. I rarely gave voice to these worries with Vince. I rarely discussed them with my parents. But talking to Liam is so incredibly easy. Words just flow, truths come out, and banter unfurls like ocean waves, softly lapping the shore. "And because of that, because I was so sure I wanted to be with her in those early days, I don't regret that I didn't figure out what I wanted to do for a living until I was older."

"When did you figure it out?"

I confess what I didn't say at IKEA. "Not till she was six or seven and going to school. At that point I'd been out of the workforce for so long I wasn't sure where to start, so I went to work for my dad because it was flexible. I could leave when I needed to at the end of the day and pick her up from school." These are things I didn't want to tell him over that lunch at IKEA. We'd just met, and I'd thought maybe they would reveal too much about me. But now I feel like we've been sharing more and it's safe to tell him. Or maybe it's because it's nighttime. Nighttime makes you braver.

"And is that when you knew you wanted to start your own company?"

I shake my head, remembering the turmoil but also the moments of clarity that eventually came. "It was a few years later. When she was ten, my dad retired, so that made the decision easier in some ways. At first, I was scared. But he helped me get set up, gave me some of his supplies and such. Still, I worried so much. I worried I'd make a mistake. I worried whether I'd be able to pull it off."

"Because of your mum? The champion worrier?" he asks, his voice gentle, thoughtful.

"You remembered," I say, a smile tugging at my lips.

"It was only a few hours ago."

"Still." I dip my head, trying to hide how much I like that he remembers what I say. I'm not used to that. Not used to someone *noticing*. I'm used to distance or obligation—those were Vince's two settings on the washing machine of his emotions. There was little in between. "And yes, my mom worried a lot when we were growing up, not just over the elliptical. She worried when my dad started his construction company." I rattle off all the what-ifs that plagued her, that she overshared with me when I was younger. "What if there's a mistake? What if something goes wrong? What if there's liability? What if we don't have business? What if it all goes belly-up? What if something happens? She was masterful at worst-case scenarios. And I took on some of those worries as an adult too. That's why it took me a while to finally do it."

"How did you push past that?" He dips his spoon into the pint one more time, then takes another bite.

"My friend Alva. I met her when our daughters became best friends in grade school. She runs the hair salon in town, and I was stressing about starting my own carpentry business. One time when she was trimming my hair, she said, 'At some point, you have to say *fuck it* to all your worries and just cut your hair off.'"

He gives a laugh, the deep belly kind. "Did you cut your hair off?"

I shake my head. "No. But her advice was the equivalent of going into a salon and asking for a wholesale change."

"Are you glad you did it?"

I nod, big and long and proud. "Absolutely. Now I'm just doing my best to keep it going. To fight for it. To say *screw the worries*. I try not to bring them home, to let them consume me. I don't want Wednesday to worry that my business might fail like I did with my parents." I swallow roughly, taking a deep breath. "Or me to worry that the business would fail because my marriage already did."

He reaches out a hand and rubs my shoulder, kind of a friendly gesture, kind of a tender one, but even so, it sends a thrill through me. It's wild and electric, because he's touching me, and I like his touch very much. "You can't beat yourself up over a relationship ending. It happens."

"But I can, and I do," I say, though talking to him is hard with his hand on my shoulder. It's hard because I want him to keep his hand there.

Or maybe not.

I want him to slide his palm everywhere.

To explore me with his hands.

With his lips.

With his body.

He squeezes harder. "Did you love him?"

That is an excellent question. But it's not hard to answer. "In college I did. At least, it felt that way. But it was also . . . *young love*. Do you know what I mean?"

A faint smile crosses his lips. "I do."

"And by the time I was pregnant, it was more like . . . this is a math problem we need to solve."

"I get that."

"And we solved it for a while. But then, I suppose the solution no longer made sense. No longer added up."

"You didn't want the same things at the same time, but you still tried to make it work, and the reality is, it would be worse if you'd stayed together just for her."

I look at him, meeting his eyes straight on, seeing so much honesty and insight in them that it thaws some part of my heart I didn't know was frozen. "Do you feel like you're doing that at all? In your quest to find Ms. Right, I mean? You're not just trying to find a mom for Ethan?"

He shakes his head, adamant. "I didn't set out to be a dad. It happened, and while I wish I had known sooner, known right away, I had to make a choice when I found out. And to make the choice to be the best I could at it." He inhales deeply. "But the thing is, I would like to find someone. I would like to be in love. I would like to know what that's like. I have no idea, but I hear it's good."

And my heart, it thunders. "You've never been in love?" The question comes out coated with emotion and maybe, just maybe, a little bit of hope.

"I don't think I have. Came close, maybe. Perhaps puppy love, but not the real thing."

"The throw-a-parade, toss-confetti, and change-your-life kind of thing?" My voice floats up, chased by that longing I seem to feel around him. A longing that grows more intense by the hour.

"Yeah, that kind." His voice is soft; his smile is gentle.

And what it does to me is insane. The flutters cascade through my body, race down my arms, rush through my cells.

Then, they double down when he adds, "I think I'd like that kind."

I. Swoon.

And I don't want to. I don't want to swoon. Or melt. Or fall.

Drawing a deep breath, I do my best to be cool, even. "You're a rare breed, Liam."

He shrugs and smiles. "Maybe I am. But what are the chances I'm going to meet someone I could love who wants the same thing at the same time? Eight billion to one?"

He sounds sadder than I've heard him before, and I try to lift his mood. "It could happen."

He lifts his spoon, offering it as a toast. "To meeting the right person in the right place at the right time."

"I will toast to that." As I clink my spoon against his, a drop of ice cream boomerangs and hits my cheek. He sets down his spoon, leans a little closer, and swipes it off my skin.

I shiver as his finger runs across my face.

And I swear, dear God, I swear that he lingers there longer than he needs to.

I swear, too, that the moon seems brighter. That the stars shine more brilliantly.

This whole moment feels like it's the right place at the right time.

Only I know it's not.

At some point later—later than I'd like to admit, since my daughter pops out at eleven with a yawn, saying she's going to bed—Liam straightens his spine, clears his throat, and hooks his thumb toward his house.

"I should go."

"Night, Mom," Wednesday says, then gives me a peck on the cheek.

"Night, Spawn."

She waves at Liam, saying good night too, but it's crushed in a yawn the size of the Grand Canyon. She pads back inside as I gather the wineglass, my e-reader, my phone, and the spoons.

"Thanks again for the ice cream."

"Thanks again for *not* giving me zucchini noodles."

I gasp. "Stay right there."

Rushing inside, I set the items on the kitchen counter, yank open the fridge, and grab the pasta salad.

I find a small glass dish, scoop some of the pasta into it, and pop on a top.

I carry it to the porch like I'm presenting him with gold-leafed chocolate. Admittedly, that's something he'd like more.

His eyes narrow. "You really love torture, don't you? Was your nickname in college The Tormentor?"

I hand him the dish. "Just try it. Before you know it, you'll be begging for radishes."

One dubious brow lifts. "Let's not get ahead of ourselves."

"C'mon. You liked the green beans."

He raises a finger. "I tolerated them."

"I bet you'll find these . . ." I hunt for the right word. "Lukewarm. I bet you'll find them lukewarmly delightful."

A laugh bursts from his chest. "All right. I'll give it a go."

He takes the dish, picks up the bag with the remains

of the ice cream, then bends closer, dusts his lips across my cheek, and says, "The best part of my date was how it started and how it ended."

My eyes float closed. A burst of longing ignites in me, a fuse about to spark.

When I open my eyes, I see everything I feel reflected back at me.

"That was my favorite part of your date too," I whisper.

For a few seconds, we stay like that, gazes locked, eyes searching, longing wrapping around us.

Like a low, steady pulse of music.

Like a waft of smoke.

It's longing stitched with wishes and wants, with desire and heat.

With things we can't have because we're out of sync.

He turns to leave.

The next morning, I find the empty dish on my porch, along with a note.

Yes, they were lukewarmly delightful. I eagerly await your next vegetable torment.

I clutch it to my chest.

So do I, Liam. So do I.

15

JANUARY

Dear Universe,

Why, oh why, did you send Liam Harris to live next door? Did you want to test my resolve? Force me to prove my mettle?

If you want to make this sweet torture up to me, please send me extra measures of resistance.

Thanks so much,
January

* * *

I try my hardest to stay strong.

Tactics include but are not limited to:

Waving like Forrest Gump when I see Liam riding his bike to work the next day.

But *not* shouting, *I want to strip off your scrubs and lick you all over.*

Flashing super-duper friendly grins every time I catch a glimpse of him.

But *not* wiggling my eyebrows and saying, *Let me torment you in other ways.*

And forcing myself to dip my head in a bucket of ice water and chant, *Do not go over there just because you saw him in his garage wearing basketball shorts while sorting through the dryer, and your eyes nearly popped out of your head on account of that gorgeous view of the finest ass you've ever seen.*

Biteable tush indeed.

Yup. I do that instead of flinging myself at him and suggesting we bang on top of the vibrating appliance.

Self-control, thy name is *moi*.

Work keeps me busy, as does back-to-school prep for Wednesday, who starts tenth grade on Monday. I finish the door for the family with the boy who thinks he's a monkey, I win the gig for Nina Clawson's boba tea shop, and I send estimates to potential clients.

I am killing it as Jackie of All Trades. Yay me.

But these sky-high levels of resistance also require support. A woman cannot survive a hot AF neighbor by willpower alone.

She requires friends.

By Sunday, I am climbing the walls for some girl-friend time, and it's coming that evening in the form of board games and beverage night, which we have occasionally. Alva sends me a check-in text that morning, and I pounce on it.

Alva: For tonight, are you thinking Candy Land and Cocktails, or Scrabble and Sangria?

January: How about Monopoly and Margaritas again? I can always go for that.

Alva: Sold. Chips and guac with that?

January: Girl, those go together like dolphins and AAA batteries.

Alva: I love your dirty mind. Speaking of, how is Prince Single Daddy Everybody Wants to Bang?

January: Ugh.

Alva: That bad?

January: That good . . . He's better than fuzzy socks.

Alva: Hold on a hot second. How long has it been since you've had sex?

January: Two years, five months, and three days.

Alva: And six hours and thirty-two seconds, but who's counting?

January: Exactly. Not me.

Alva: It's probably time for an intervention. Want an

escort?

January: Yes, that's all I've ever wanted. Send one now, please.

Alva: On his way. Until then, I'm just going to gently remind you that comparing a hot man to socks means you have completely forgotten how to ride a bike.

January: I have. I won't even try to deny it. But in my defense, I haven't forgotten how to work the dolphin.

Alva: And is Prince Fuzzy Socks starring in your dolphin dreams?

January: He is the lead actor, the supporting actor, the cameraman, the tech crew, and the sound engineer. And I have no regrets.

Alva: You should never regret your dolphin fantasies. But is he appearing in other dreams?

January: Sigh. Yes. In my dating dreams. And I don't want to have those. I don't want to have those at all! Make them stop.

Alva: Girl, I think we need to talk.

* * *

When I pop into her salon later that day during a break between appointments, Alva shoots me a *come to your bestie* smile. But as I slump down in the red chair in front of the mirror, I'm not sure what to say.

Other than what's become brutally obvious.

"I like my neighbor," I confess.

She squeezes my shoulders. "I know, sweetie. I know."

16

LIAM

On Sunday night, after Ethan slips into the land of Nod, I wander through my new home like a dog unsure where to settle.

I push open the back door, head down the steps, and flick on the pool lights. Flopping down on a lounge chair, I swipe to an audiobook on my phone, trying to zone in on the power of virality.

I keep rewinding the first five minutes on exponential growth, but I can't bloody focus, on account of staring over the fence and wishing my neighbor would appear.

I go back inside. Gritting my teeth, I tell myself not to pop out onto the front porch just so I can swing my gaze left and see if she's home.

I remind myself I don't need to wander down the driveway and check the mail.

It's Sunday night. There is no fucking mail.

I issue a restraining order against me going to the guest room just to straighten the blinds on the window that looks out on her kitchen, where I can sometimes see a sliver of her when she's at the sink.

I don't do any of those things, because I'm not a stalker.

Or a creeper.

Or that kind of guy.

Also, there's no furniture in my guest room, so it'd be really obvious that I was spying.

Instead, I retreat to my bedroom and slump down on my bed with the black cover, flashing back to January's comments on my monochromatic color scheme.

A smile bends my lips as I remember the day I met her.

How fiery and fun she was.

How outgoing and welcoming she was.

How easy to talk to she was.

She's still all of those things.

And we're two trains chugging in opposite directions.

I reach for my wallet and flip it open. Sliding out the card from Valeria Rodriquez, I replay my brief ice cream encounter with her.

The sparkless one.

But that's not her fault.

Perhaps we'll find that magic in person.

When *we* talk.

When *we* connect.

It can happen, surely.

And I can do this.

I can absolutely do this.

After all, dating, searching, and hopefully finding that special someone is my big goal, after helping my dad.

And since I'm doing just fine on that first one, it's time to stay the course on the second.

I text her.

* * *

On Monday morning, Ethan and I hop on our bikes and ride down Mallard Lane, then along the next one, making our way to Duck Falls Elementary. When we reach the school, he parks his bike in the rack and shoulders his backpack, then gives me a salute and says, "Okay, you can go now."

I laugh. "Were you worried I'd cramp your style?"

He shrugs. "Kind of."

I punch him on the shoulder. "Glad I've raised you to be so independent at the ripe old age of nine."

"Nine and four-fifths."

"Hello? Arithmetic, please. You turn ten in a month."

"Nine and eleven-twelfths."

"Well done. Thank you." I roll my eyes, then grab my phone, holding it up. "Pic for Aunt Jane and Oliver?"

"Sure," he says, giving a smile for the camera, then he whirls around and calls out, "Also, you look clean."

"All without any white sneakers."

I send the first-day-of-school pic to my New York friends and family, then hop back on my bike and wheel away, heading to The Good Egg. It's a cute little breakfast café just off the Duck Falls town square, where I've arranged to meet Valeria for a quick breakfast date.

A breakfast date that might lead to sparks.

A man can hope.

A man in pursuit of Ms. Right can dream indeed.

When I arrive, I park the bike outside and lock it up, then head inside and grab a booth, looking around as I wait.

Does January ever come here?

Does she pop in on Mondays?

Would she order the veggie omelet? Maybe make a joke about tormenting me with peppers? Then I'd tell her I actually love peppers—red, orange, and yellow.

But not green. Never green.

Bet that'd surprise her but make her roll her sky-blue eyes too.

A ray of warmth spreads over my skin as I imagine that conversation, having it with her. Here, or at her home, or mine.

The bell tinkles above the door, and for a sliver of a second, I imagine it's her.

In her pink work shirt.

In Timberlands.

With that crooked grin.

Those birds peeking out of the sleeves of her shirt.

Picking up a to-go order but deciding to join me instead.

But as my eyes laser in on the woman walking through the doorway, I sit up straighter, conducting a full mind sweep.

Erase all thoughts of other women from your brain now.

I catalog my date. Toned arms on display in a light-blue sundress, freckles splashed across her nose, hair in a braid.

A smile that's inviting.

I stand. "Hello, Valeria." Awkwardness kicks in for a few seconds. Do I drop a kiss on her cheek, give her a hug, or clap her on the back?

I don't normally feel awkward on dates.

But then, I'm not normally thinking about other women when I'm on dates.

Do what you'd do if you were having breakfast with Summer.

A quick, chaste hug wins.

We sit, open the menus, and peruse the offerings.

After the waitress takes our order—eggs and potatoes for me, while my date chooses French toast—Valeria sets her hands on the table and shoots me a warm smile again. "I have to admit, I have a bit of a sweet tooth. I can't resist French toast for breakfast or cereal for dinner. And I guess that's why I'm in the ice cream business."

And how about that? We have something in common right away—a shared sweet tooth.

Must latch on to this commonality. "Honestly, it's a daily battle for me not to have French toast and cereal for every meal as well."

She laughs, then we chat a little bit more about our favorite treats.

It's rather innocuous. It's mostly fun. Surely this is the start of a good date.

She's easy to talk to. She's quick-witted. And we seem to have enough to say to each other.

But there's one big, glaring problem.

One huge, massive issue.

She's not January.

At the end of the date, I'm not entirely sure what to do.

I should want to go on another date with her.

But I don't.

So I stay the course, pretending she's Summer, or any female friend.

Nothing wrong with friendship, right?

Except I get the sense from her body language, from the way she leans a little closer and parts her lips the slightest bit, that she wants more than friendship. That she wants a second date.

As she finishes her French toast, she says with a flirty tone, "I know a great place with chocolate chip pancakes. We could try that next."

My stomach nose-dives.

Because I'm going to need to tell this smart, fun, lively woman that this is going nowhere.

My interest is elsewhere.

All my sparks are lit by someone else.

Someone who doesn't have the same dreams, the same goals, or the same five-year plan as I do.

I brace myself to end this before it starts.

After I pay for breakfast, I say, "This was fun. It reminds me of going out to breakfast with my friend Summer in New York City."

Two lines form above Valeria's nose, a telltale crease

in her brow that says she didn't want to be friend-zoned. But then she erases it quickly, gives me a smile, and says, "Friends. Perfect. That's what I was thinking too."

I beam. Whew. Maybe I read her all wrong. Or maybe she's simply cool with a guy being up-front about what he wants and what he doesn't want. Either way, I'm glad I was able to be clear and kind. It's a small town. Everyone knows everyone.

"Great, then," I say, and now I know what to do. I extend a hand to shake.

She shakes back. "Thanks for breakfast, and if I run into you here again, we can have a friendly . . . chocolate croissant."

"Sounds perfect," I say, and on the way to work, my phone buzzes.

It's Missy, confirming our lunch date for tomorrow.

Missy, who doesn't like fish.

Missy, who's outgoing and friendly.

Missy, who January knows.

Dammit.

When I reach the Lucky Falls office, my vet tech tells me a little brown terrier is on her way. "Blossom has a terrible bee allergy, and she was stung this morning on her walk."

That's all I need to extricate dates and women from my mind. Minutes later, the cutie-pie arrives with a swollen face and a worried person.

I administer the necessary shot for the little sweetie, reassuring the owner that her darling Blossom will be fine, and that she won't look like an overgrown shar-pei for very long.

For the next few hours, the prospect of dating and faking it is forgotten, but later the charade weighs on me like an anchor tugging me down.

It makes me start to question all the things I thought I wanted when I moved here just a few weeks ago.

* * *

Missy is funny.

At least, I think so.

I've done a serviceable job of paying attention to her over tea during my lunch break the next day.

The willowy redhead chatters on about the time she bumped into a wall in the yarn shop because she was checking out a brown-and-tan Chihuahua walking by outside the store.

"I was like this." She demonstrates by smacking the air in front of her as hard as one can possibly smack air. She shrugs a shoulder, saying with humor, "That'll teach the store to put a wall in the way when I'm trying to stare shamelessly at all the dogs walking by."

"Walls should be removed when cute pooches stroll the streets," I say, a little deadpan, and she laughs too. She doesn't take herself too seriously, facile with a dry sense of humor, my favorite kind.

But it's January's favorite kind too.

January's quite good at dishing out the dry, the droll, and the deadpan.

She's good at dishing out vegetables too, and that's

not something I thought I would enjoy, but I definitely like them coming from her.

She's also great at serving up honesty and open-heartedness. Our conversations have been the kind that can spill endlessly into the night.

"Some are definitely hard to resist," Missy says, and I blink, reorienting myself to the moment.

Hard to resist?

Like my neighbor?

Wait. No. That's wrong.

We're talking about dogs that are hard to resist staring at, not neighbors who are hard to resist talking to, thinking about, and wanting to kiss.

Wanting to kiss all over. Wanting to taste, to savor, to *please*.

Taking a drink of my tea, I zero in on the woman in front of me. The woman who is taking the time out of her day to go on a date with me. The woman who popped over from Duck Falls to have a meal. I want to be respectful of her and keep my mind and heart open to all of the possibilities.

Since the possibilities won't happen with the woman commandeering my thoughts.

"Tell me what you like about Duck Falls, Missy," I say to the redhead.

She talks about all the little things, like the glitter on the sidewalks and the ducks in their pink wading ponds, then the sheer number of women-owned businesses. "We like to joke that somehow Athena is responsible for the town. No one can really figure out why there are so many more women here than men. It doesn't actually make any sense."

"Magic?" I suggest playfully. "Also, I'm absolutely not complaining that there are more women here than men."

Missy flashes me a bright smile. "I bet that doesn't bother you in the least."

This is the moment when a date *should* tip over into flirting. Into banter. Into talk about being good in bed or banging in the kitchen, like January and I teased each other about at the IKEA café.

Yet I can't seem to sit on that end of the seesaw with Missy. Don't want to tilt it in the direction of innuendo.

Because I don't actually want to have that banter with anybody other than my neighbor, and that is getting to be a problem.

I'm three dates into my quest, and already my stupid heart craves exactly what it can't have.

"I just love Duck Falls," Missy continues, wrapping her hands around her iced vanilla latte. "I love all of the ducks, the people, and the train tracks, and I love the women-owned businesses, like the yarn shop and the bookstore and the hair salon and the carpenter."

I sit up straighter, keying in on that, like a dog cocking his head when his person opens a bag of kibble. "Carpenter?" I ask, doing my best to seem casually interested.

Not deeply, intensely, ridiculously interested.

"You know! Your next-door neighbor. January. She's the best. She actually started our board game and beverage nights."

I try to suppress a grin that threatens to take over my whole face. Now this date is getting interesting. This date is going where I want. Perhaps *Missy* is my dating insider, about to serve up details on the woman next door. Details I want to gobble up. "What's board game and beverages?" I ask, as if I'm only mildly intrigued by that tidbit, when I am fascinated with every morsel.

"It's a really cool club for the female business owners of the town. We all try to get together once a month, and we play board games and have beverages. The whole group of us—me as the lingerie shop owner, and then Alva, who owns the hair salon, and Nina with the boba tea shop. And the best part is we make up crazy rules on the fly. Like, a couple of weeks ago, we were all playing Monopoly, and January had this funny idea," Missy says, and I'm on the edge of my seat, elbows on the table, eyes wide open, ears pricked. I'm listening to every word because I want to soak in everything there is to know about my next-door neighbor.

"Alva was being a total stickler, so we thought it would be so much more fun if we randomly banded together and bought groups of properties and charged her higher rent when she landed on them," Missy says, grinning the whole time.

"And that was January's idea?"

She nods vigorously. "She's just like that. It's *so* her personality. We were drinking and toasting and mostly poking fun at Alva, and then January started tossing all the money at us, saying she was going to open a club and she was making it rain, making it rain," Missy recounts, and I'm so ridiculously delighted with this story that I cannot wait to see January later and ask her all about her board game night.

That is all I want.

Plain and simple.

* * *

Since Mum invited us for supper that evening, Ethan and I pop home after school and work, then head to their place in Lucky Falls before I have a chance to give January grief about making it rain Monopoly money.

Over chicken enchiladas, my dad peppers me with questions. "And what about Kate Stevenson's dog? How's Freddie doing with his heart condition?"

I update my dad on the golden retriever he treated for eight years. He gives me some suggestions—they are exactly what I told the client, but I simply nod and say, "Yes, that's great advice. I'll tell her that."

It makes him happy to stay involved like this. It keeps his brain fresh. I can only imagine that as his world is narrowing, becoming blurrier by the day, it must mean so much to him to still be able to use his mind.

But the thing is, I don't actually need my father's advice on how to handle a dog's heart condition. Instead, I need his wisdom on the condition of mine.

After dinner, I pull him aside, setting a hand on his arm so that I can guide him through the living room toward the back deck. We step outside.

"There's something else I want to talk to you about, Dad."

He gives me a crisp nod, sliding into that fatherly zone that he's so good at occupying. "What is it, Liam?"

I tell him a little bit about my dilemma, a little bit about how I've been feeling, a little bit about what I want.

He takes a deep breath, the kind that says, *Wow, you've got quite a conundrum there.*

But then the soft smile that draws up his lips, the thoughtful glint in his eyes, tells me that this impromptu bonding session is a riddle he wants to unravel. "I think the key is you should be honest. That's what matters most. Be up-front with the woman you saw today. And be up-front with the other one too, even if it's as complicated as you say it is," he says.

We talk a little more, then I clap him on the shoulder. "You've always steered me in the right direction, Dad."

He shakes his head. "No. You've always known what direction to go. All you needed was someone to remind you of what you're already feeling here." He taps my sternum.

When Ethan and I leave, I let his advice sink in, slide under my skin, invade my brain.

I let it roll around in my cells.

Be up-front.

Be honest.

I have been, but not all the way, not with every woman.

And I need to be. Because I know where I want to

be, even though taking a chance isn't part of my plan, or the great dating escapade, and it won't likely align with my goals, my dreams, or my five-year plan.

But I can't seem to want anything else.

And there's a right way to do things, and a wrong way to do things. Whether this is a big town or a small town, there's only one way to do the *next* thing.

Once I'm home, I don't text Missy.

Texting a woman who unexpectedly fed you nuggets of information about another woman is for cowards.

Calling is the only way to do it. I ring her up.

"Hi, Liam. Good to hear from you."

"Hi, Missy. I had a great time at lunch," I say, pacing in my kitchen, readying myself to say something I didn't plan to say, because I didn't expect to feel it.

Or rather, I didn't want to.

"I did too. You're a hoot," she says.

I swallow, then finish. "And one of the reasons I had such a great time is because you shared so many terrific details about January."

"Oh." That one syllable is laced with confusion.

And I'm about to unlace it.

"It seems I've developed a fondness for my next-door neighbor," I say, opting for a little old-fashioned flare, just because Missy seems like someone who enjoys more of the story.

And it seems to work, because Missy is squealing.

"Yes! You'd be adorable together. I'm so excited. She deserves someone like you. I'm rooting for you two."

I smile at her reaction—her very Missy, very enthusiastic reaction. "Thanks. I don't have any idea what will happen, if anything. And nothing has."

"Well, change that now, doc," she says, in an over-the-top bawdy voice. "Make it rain, make it rain, make it rain."

Laughing, I say, "I'll see what I can do."

She clears her throat, going more serious. "Are you going to ask her out on a date?"

I give her the only answer I can.

* * *

I tell Ethan to get ready for bed, and I go next door, knocking on January's door.

When she answers, her chestnut hair piled in a messy bun, her pink T-shirt stained with plaster, I raise my hands in surrender. "I'm willing to eat radishes if you tell me all about your board game club."

A smile races across her lips, as Wednesday cackles from the couch, pokes her head up, and says, "You should hear how crazy competitive they got Sunday night when they played Monopoly again. They're so loud I can't even sleep when she has board game club. But Monopoly is nothing compared to how rowdy they are with Candy Land."

January swings open the door, invites me in, and tells me more about the board game nights. I eat up every detail.

But I can't linger, since Ethan has school tomorrow, and a bedtime.

I hook my thumb in the direction of my house. "I

should go, but thanks for entertaining me with your tawdry tales," I say, girding myself to say more, to ask for what I want.

"Thanks for demanding them." She looks at the clock on her kitchen wall. "Tomorrow is furniture assembly night. Are you ready?"

I rub my palms together. "Ready to sit on my arse and watch you do all the work."

She nudges me with her elbow. "I will put you to work as my assistant."

That sounds like more fun than it should be. It sounds, too, like exactly what I want.

"Fine. If you insist," I say as we walk to the door then onto her porch. The night air has cooled, but a summer breeze drifts by in the dark, as the starlit sky and the porch light illuminate her face.

"I do insist."

"And I am looking forward to it. I arranged for Goodwill to pick up my bachelor pad furniture tomorrow morning."

"Perfect."

My feet feel like they're stuck here, and I don't want to leave. I won't leave until I say what I came to say.

This is the chance.

It's time to take it.

For all that it's unexpected.

That it might derail my plans.

It's time, because she's the one I want to invite to a wine bar, a breakfast café, a tea shop.

I go for it. "Do you want to have dinner afterward?"

Her eyes go wide and vulnerable. There's a twitch in

her lips too, as if they're curving up of their own accord. "Do you mean out or at your house?"

There's a question in her question.

I take another chance, answering from the heart, full of my feelings for her, and full of my desire too. "Why don't we have dinner at my house?"

After all, Ethan is spending a few hours at Kerri's.

January licks her lips, nods, and says yes. I have no idea what I've just gotten myself into, but I can't wait.

17

JANUARY

Wednesday—the day, not my kid—is a light one for me.

I only have one job scheduled, fixing some hinges in a winery this morning, so I'm planning on spending the rest of the day on billing.

But who am I kidding?

I'll probably spend my time daydreaming of tonight with Liam while I try to wade through invoices.

In the morning, I brew a pot of coffee, pour a cup, then send my kid on her way to school.

"Learn lots of things. Make good choices. Don't hack any of your teachers' accounts," I say, walking her to the door.

She raises a brow. "Not even my algebra teacher's? Because word on the street is he made a cool mil on some tech funds, so I bet he'd be worth a hack."

"Hmm." I allow the corner of my lips to turn up. "That one is fine. Go for it."

She pumps a fist dramatically. "Yes!"

"But cover your tracks, 'kay?"

With an eye roll, she says, "Duh. Obviously."

I give her a smooch on the forehead. "So proud of you."

"I'll see you . . . what time did you want me home?"

A flush crawls up my chest, knowing why I asked her to go to Audrey's for dinner. "Eight would be fantastic," I say, my voice a little dry.

"How about eight-thirty?" Her tone is hopeful, like she's the one asking for something I don't want to give.

I suppress a wicked grin. "Sure. If you must."

"Thanks, Spawner."

"See ya, Spawn."

I wave as she heads down the steps and walks to school about a mile away. Along the route, she'll meet up with Audrey, and they'll amble together, planning their next quirky food test for YouTube.

I make my own way down the steps, then stop at my vegetable gardens out front, checking on the greens, taking a drink of my coffee, and enjoying the late August sun warming my shoulders and warming my soul.

And I know why.

Because my mind is on tonight.

My body is reaching for this evening.

My whole being reaches for possibilities, for chances.

I said yes, knowing the danger. Knowing the risk—the risk of capsizing the life I've carved out in this town.

He's my neighbor.

I have to see him every day. I have a kid who's happy. A business that's growing. Friends who support me.

Do I truly want to risk all of that for a roll in the hay?

For a dinner?

For a night with him?

He wants more. He wants a future. He wants a Mrs.

I want none of that.

I want my life. The one I'm finally having.

Why, then, did I say yes?

As I survey the green beans in my garden, I flash back to last night.

To how I felt when he came over. When he asked me to have dinner.

A giddy sensation whirls through me out of nowhere.

I set a hand on my belly, smiling.

That's why I said yes.

Because of that feeling—a little dizzy, a little drunk. But it's a good dizzy, a good drunk.

And he's a good man.

I can manage whatever this is. Whatever tonight becomes. We're mature, responsible adults. Surely we won't be the first neighbors in the history of the world to act on an attraction, then tuck it away and return to the way we were.

Yes, that's how we will do it.

We will do it the smart way.

The adult way.

The *can I still borrow a cup of sugar in a year's time* way.

Almost as if he can read my thoughts, I hear his voice.

"Fancy meeting you here."

I turn to find the most handsome, charmingly sarcastic man I've ever met wandering across his yard toward mine, holding a cup of tea. I stand, unable to wipe the flirty smile from my face. He's so delectable in his blue scrubs as I catalog his features. His freshly shaven jaw, his deep brown eyes, his toned arms.

And most of all, his smile. Confident, happy, and genuine.

My stomach flips.

"Such a shock to see me outside in my front yard, isn't it?" I ask.

"Are you sure you're not stalking me?"

I arch a brow. "I was going to say the same thing to you."

He laughs. "Guilty as charged, then."

"Might as well slap the handcuffs on me too."

His eyes light up, like they're awash with dirty thoughts. Maybe we're both being totally honest. Maybe we're both saying damn the risks because . . . this desire is powerful. "I'm amenable to that," he murmurs.

Those soulful brown irises darken, and a current zaps through me. I want to rope my arms around him and beg him to kiss me soft, then hard, so hard it'd be like he was fucking me with his mouth.

Shit.

I need to get it together.

"I'm working from home most of the day," I offer, simply to say something besides *Take me to bed.*

In a heartbeat, his expression shifts from playful and to practical. "The furniture delivery is coming by around eleven. I thought I would be able to be home for it, but I have to . . ." He makes a snipping gesture with his hands.

"Ah. You are relieving a dog of his most prized possessions."

"I am."

"Do you want me to let them in?"

"Would you?" He sounds as if I just said I'll deliver him chocolate from Paris every day for the rest of his life.

"I'd be happy to. That is, if you're comfortable giving me a key."

He taps his chin. "That's a good question. Are you planning on rifling through all my drawers?"

"Just the interesting ones, like your sock drawer."

"Oh, by all means, go right ahead, then. If you want to find the really fascinating stuff, don't forget the utensil drawer. It's to the right of the dishwasher."

"Thanks for the tip. I've been meaning to look at your spoons. Spoons tell you so much about a man."

"Don't forget to check out the knives, then, too. That should tell you everything you need to know."

I crack up, loving that the man gives such clever innuendo. "And perhaps your nightstand drawer?"

He growls, a low, sexy rumble. "Perhaps yours."

I tug at the neck of my T-shirt. "You'd find . . . very interesting things."

Another groan emanates from his throat, so damn sexy. "You're making it very hard to go to work."

"Am I?" I ask, unable to resist this dive well past innuendo and straight into naughty land.

"Yes, but Sparky the Wonder Pup has been fasting all morning, so I can't leave him hanging."

"Pun intended."

"Pun always intended." He scratches his jaw, exhaling. "I'll leave a key under the mat. Thank you for helping me. You're an angel."

"You think I'm an angel?" I ask, jutting out my hip the slightest bit.

"Are you telling me you're a devil instead, January?" His question comes out a little husky, a little smoky. I step closer, getting into his space. I want to feel the vibrations between us, the energy that seems to be intensifying by the second. When he asked me to dinner last night, it's as if that unleashed all of the unacknowledged heat between us, and now we're reveling in it.

"Do I seem like one?"

He inches closer too. "I'd like to know the devil in you."

"You want to know if I'm good or bad?"

His lips part. His eyes darken. His Adam's apple bobs. This sexy, kind, outgoing, clever man looks absolutely undone.

A gust of air crosses his lips, and it is clear what's happening tonight. "I do want to know, absolutely," he says in a whisper that makes me feel as undone as he looks.

But he has to go to work. And so I vow to surprise him.

* * *

I handle the delivery.

But I don't stop there. I don't simply let the guys in and leave. I need something to keep myself busy today.

Rather than wait and assemble the furniture later, I do it all now. I put everything together, focusing the whole time on the task, blasting my new playlist as I put together the couch, the table, and the chair. Four hours later, everything is assembled. I'm sweating, and my muscles are tired, but it's a good sweat and it's a good tired.

Nothing a shower won't cure.

I pick up all my tools, straighten up, and then grab a sheet of paper and leave him a note.

Am I an angel? Let's find out.

I go home. I shower. I put on a pink sundress. He likes me in pink. But more than that, I like me in pink. I like, too, how all my ink is on display, how he can see the birds flying up my arm.

Well, not *all* of my ink.

I smile privately as I wait for him to return from work, keeping myself busy making a salad I hope he'll like.

Or at least tolerate.

Around six there's a knock on my door. I open it, drawing a sharp, fevered breath when I take in a freshly showered Liam in jeans and a gray T-shirt that's nice and snug across his pecs, showing off his strong arms. He stares shamelessly at me, then unleashes an appreciative *wow* as he holds up two bottles of wine.

"You're an angel for the furniture. Thank you. Thank you so incredibly much. But I'd like to know both sides of you. First, would you like wine?" It comes out gravelly, like the question isn't about wine. It's about desire. It's about tonight.

"I would." I point to the white. "But I want it later."

"And what do you want now?"

I feel breathless, jittery all over, but ready too—knowing the danger, knowing the risk.

Knowing, too, that if I'm going to adult this thing with him, then the adulting needs to start before we get naked.

I meet his gaze. "This doesn't change anything, does it?"

"Not if we don't let it," he says, his eyes never straying from mine.

"Then let's *not* let it change things."

He raises the bottle. "I'll drink to that." He tips his head toward his house. "Come over, January. Come over now."

He's never sounded this commanding.

This determined.

His voice makes me hot, turns me on.

I grab the salad, step onto the porch, and shut the door behind me. He sets a hand on my back, making me shiver, making me want.

The second we're inside his house, he takes the salad

bowl, sets it on the entryway table, and puts down the bottles of wine.

When he shuts the door, he pushes me up against it.

18

LIAM

Screw food.

Fuck wine.

Forget everything in the world right now but *this*.

There are no questions. There is no uncertainty. We are about to kiss.

January is an inevitability.

A gorgeous, fiery fait accompli.

But even if I'm dead certain that our lips are about to connect, that our bodies are going to crash together, I'll still savor every second of this. Whether it's a done deal or not, whether this kiss comes as a surprise or it doesn't, I intend to relish it.

Because a first kiss is *always* a surprise.

It's a delicious, decadent discovery.

Will she like it slow, fast, and deep? Long, hard, and wet?

Will it be an exploration? A revelation? A declaration?

Will it sizzle? Will it make my head go hazy?

The second the door shuts, I spin her around and back her into the door.

Her eyes flare with heat. Mine roam up and down her body. "Have I told you how much I appreciate what you did in my house today?"

"No. Not entirely. Do you want to show me?" She asks it all flirty, full of intention, and her forthrightness is a massive turn-on.

"I do. I very much want to show you all of my appreciation," I say, as my right hand finds her waist and curls around it.

I savor the contact.

That first electric moment of touching her sends a wave of heat crashing over me.

Her blue eyes shimmer. Her lips part. Her breath catches. She's in this as much as I am, and that ratchets up my lust another hundred degrees. My pulse roars just from being near her like this, and yet I want to get so much closer. I move against her, barely a breath between us.

"Confession. I thought about this the day I met you."

She swallows, her expression full of dirty wonder. "You did?"

"You didn't?" I ask, laughing.

She laughs too. And I love this about us. I love that we *get* each other. I love that our laughter gels and that we can be like this, firing innuendos, teasing each other, wanting each other.

"Then do it," she whispers.

"Gladly, *neighbor*," I say, like the word tastes delicious on my tongue.

I bring my face down to hers, wanting to kiss her, but wanting to draw it out too, to make her shiver, to make her shudder.

I brush my lips along the column of her neck. "Actually, from the second I met you, I wanted to kiss you."

She shudders against me. "I felt it too. Wanted it too."

I brush my lips against her ear, nipping her delicious earlobe. She tastes fantastic, and she smells even better, all clean and pretty, like some kind of flowery lotion that absolutely drives me crazy. It's a sweet, feminine scent that spells *woman*.

A woman who knows her mind. Who knows her wants.

The scent wraps around me. It intoxicates me. I lick her ear, my tongue coasting across the shell of it. "Thought about you all day."

"Including while you were snipping dogs?"

I chuckle. "Let us not discuss snipping while my dick is hard."

On that note, she pushes her pelvis against the outline of my erection, and I groan. Savagely.

My head goes hazy as the need to touch her everywhere intensifies, thrumming through my veins.

My lips travel across her jaw, sucking and kissing as I go, and when I think I can't take it anymore—the tease, the buildup—she's gasping and murmuring. Her sounds send adrenaline coursing through my body. My skin grows hotter, and every cell in my body craves the woman in my arms.

I am so damn lucky to have her here in my house, wanting all the same things I do.

And I want her to know with how I touch her, how I taste her, how I plan to bring her oceans of pleasure that she deserves it all.

She deserves everything.

I capture her lips with mine, and we kiss like everything makes sense in the world.

Like this kiss is the answer to all the questions.

Like everything we've ever needed to know can be found in the way our lips fuse together.

We explore each other's lips. The feel and the taste of her floods my senses, fills my mind, spreads across my entire body. As the kiss deepens, the need to touch her more—here, there, everywhere—escalates. I slide my hands up her arms, cupping her cheeks. Holding her beautiful face in my hands.

Everything feels right about this moment.

We are the picture of wanting, needing, and *having*.

My tongue slides into her waiting mouth, and we moan as we connect. We murmur as we explore. My hands slide into her lush hair, and hers climb up my chest, rubbing against my pecs in a way that shows she likes what she feels. So much so it seems like she melts into the kiss. And soon, this becomes a long, slow moment, and we're both gasping for air as our hands and bodies seek each other.

We press and touch and grind. Heat radiates between us as we go for another round of kissing, deep and fevered this time, teeth and tongues and fingers in hair, then grappling against clothes.

I feel wild. And I want to share all that wildness with her. To let her go wild too, since I'm pretty sure that's exactly how she'll be in bed.

I break the kiss.

"That's only the beginning of how much I appreciate you," I say, all rough and gravelly because I can't speak any other way right now, since she's fried all my brain cells. She's frazzled everything inside me, and I want her so much.

Her eyes are wicked, rimmed with lust. "But then, how else do you appreciate me?"

This woman. I'm going to show her. I turn her around, admiring the view of her back, the curve of her ass, the shape of those strong legs. "Hands against the door."

She lets out a sexy purr, sliding her palms up the wood.

"Let me show you," I say, moving her hands up higher so those inked arms stretch above her body, her sparrows soaring to the ceiling.

She glances back at me. "So this is how we're doing it?"

"Yes, this is how we're going to do it. Because I have a thing for your neck."

I move her hair to the side, and I kiss the back of her neck, sliding my lips across her delicious skin. The moan she unleashes is like the gorgeous chorus to a song, and I want to hear it again and again, so I kiss her more and more.

No. It's *worship.*

She moves like water, almost swaying, bending,

curving against me as my lips travel along her flesh to her shoulder, then to her collarbone and back up. This time I don't simply kiss her. I nibble.

Her breath catches, a long, needy pant. Another bite, another moan that spurs me on.

As I push the strap of her dress down her arm, licking and nipping across her skin, her delicious scent goes to my head with every single stroke of my lips.

I kiss down her back to the top of her dress, tugging it down a little farther, flicking my tongue along her spine. The whole time she wriggles against me, arching, moaning.

But her dress is in the way.

I solve that problem by reaching for the hem, lifting it up, then pulling it over her head and tossing it onto the couch that she built earlier today.

I let out a long, appreciative moan as I regard the gorgeous beauty in front of me. She wears only a cotton bra and knickers. Her long, lovely, luxurious back is on display.

I run a finger along her spine, and she shivers as I touch her. "Your back is incredible," I say.

"Then maybe put your mouth on it."

"You love to give directions," I say.

"I just know what I want. And I want you touching me. I want you kissing me."

"Good thing I want my mouth all over you," I say, as I savor every single second of tasting her. Moaning, she writhes against me and makes her desire known as I kiss down to the waistband of her knickers, tugging at them, dusting my lips over the top of the gorgeous globes of her ass until she spins around, all wild and needy. She gestures at me, pulling at my T-shirt. "Off. I want your clothes off."

"What do you know? I want my clothes off too." And then I cup her chin, bring her mouth next to mine, and whisper against her, "I fucking love that you know your mind."

"I do. And I want you to have me and touch me and kiss me and eat me and fuck me."

That sounds like a perfect dinner plan. I lift her up and let her koala me, wrapping her legs around my waist, her arms around my neck. As I walk to my bedroom, her body twined around mine, I tease her, saying, "But what about dinner?"

Her grin is dirty and flirty. "Eat me first."

"You first. Dinner later. Sounds like the perfect recipe."

Because there's really no argument ever in the history of the universe against doing exactly what the woman wants in bed. Especially when it's exactly what I want too.

In the bedroom, I lower her to the mattress and strip off her bra, then I delight in those fantastic breasts, savoring each one, lavishing attention on her nipples. I kiss my way down her body as she moves under me, panting and groaning. When I reach the top of the white scrap of fabric, she is the most beautiful sight ever as she twists on my bed, lifting her hips, asking for more. For more touch. For more connection.

"Off. Take them off."

"Why, yes. That's exactly what I planned to do." I

slide the last shred of clothing off her. Heat bursts inside me, like a fire roaring through my veins, as I gaze at the stunning sight in front of me.

January, totally aroused, completely naked, glisteningly wet.

And there's one more treat too.

The answer to a question I had when I first noticed the art on her arms. Does she have any under her clothes, out of sight?

The answer is yes.

A delicate tulip graces her hip bone. Pink and green, and so very lovely. I breathe out hard, tracing the tiny flower with my index finger. "This is you," I say reverently.

She nods, a knowing smile crossing her lips. "Yes. It's me."

"This is the girlie girl in your tomboy. It's the sexy, sweet, feminine side under all that fix-it, do-it-yourself hotness."

"Yes," she says, that one syllable full of delight, like she loves that I figured this out, discovered this about her.

I bring my mouth to her hip, press a soft kiss to the tulip, and lick the delicate lines of it. A murmur falls from her lips, and when I raise my face, I ask another question. "When did you get it?"

"Almost two years ago." It comes out as a whisper, at a low volume, underscoring the secret she's sharing. "No one's seen it."

A fresh rush of lust whips through me, but it's more than desire. It's stronger, richer already. Since she's sharing herself with me in a way she hasn't with anyone else in ages. She is a gift, and she doesn't give herself easily.

She deserves to be cherished, so I kiss the tulip once more, like I am cherishing it. I kiss it, murmuring against it, "Beautiful."

Then I rise up, meet her gaze, and say, "Thank you for showing me your art."

There's so much more to that statement than the words themselves, and I think she knows it.

"Thank you for seeing it," she whispers, and for several heady seconds, it feels like we're teetering on the edge of a dangerous cliff.

One that leads to jagged rocks and thorny terrain.

But before we fall, she catches us with her body. She moves up onto her elbows and looks at me, desire in her eyes. "Why don't you at least take off your shirt?"

I do as she asks, peeling it off, tossing it onto the floor, and here we are, back firmly on the physical plane, and that's fine by me. "Don't ask me to take anything else off, because I need to have my mouth between your legs right the hell now."

She moans and answers with the most wonderful word: "Yes."

I set my hands on her knees and spread her open, my pulse spiking. When my lips kiss her hot, wet center, my eyes roll back in my head at the first luscious taste of her. At the sweetness of her desire.

And the sounds she makes.

Moans, groans, sighs.

Murmurs, long and plaintive.

My name too—how it turns into a cry and an arch as she bows her back.

She's wildly desperate already.

I kiss her, flicking my tongue against the delicious rise of her clit, moaning at the decadence of her. My dick throbs harder in my jeans, and lust spins through my veins because she tastes spectacular. She sounds even better, panting, and babbling the most gorgeous noises ever.

Like a woman who wants everything I'm giving her. Who's saying my name. Who's saying, *"More."* Who's pulling me closer.

She tastes like a woman who wants everything. Who wants me. Who wants to come very, very soon.

She spreads her legs wider then threads her hands through my hair, yanking me closer as she chants, "Don't stop. I'm close. I'm almost there."

Seconds later, she bucks against my face and lets out a long, keening moan. Her hands slide up into her own hair, and she's touching herself. It's the most gorgeous thing in the world as she comes hard on my lips.

Shouting, crying, and losing her mind, it seems.

And I am ridiculously happy that I could do that for her. As well as insanely aroused.

As she comes down, I break the contact, slide my jeans off, find a condom quickly, and sheath myself.

And then I ask a most important question. "What would it take to get you there a second time?"

She stares at me. Licks her lips. "Just your cock."

"Well, I was hoping you would say that, but what position is best for you?"

Sitting up, she grabs my dick, tugging me to her.

I don't need to give the position a second thought, because she's issued her declaration.

I slide into the woman who occupies my thoughts, my body lighting up from the hot, tight grip of her.

From the noises she makes.

From the feel of her as I fill her.

She knows exactly what she wants. Sliding her knees up to her chest, she moves them higher, near her breasts.

Offering me herself.

For pleasure.

For both of us.

Shamelessly.

And I fucking love it.

"Can you give it to me hard, Liam? Make me feel you everywhere," she whispers.

My brain short-circuits. Lust fries all the cells in my body. I thrust deeper, push her right knee higher. "Like that? Just like that?"

Her features twist in some kind of ecstatic agony. "Yes, just like that." It's a breathy, needy answer tinged with relief, like she's been craving this kind of intimacy, this kind of sex.

Pressing a hand against her knee, I go deeper, so she can feel me both in her and against her, where she needs me. "I happen to be quite good at following directions," I whisper against her cheek, then laugh lightly. "Well, when it comes to sex and recipes."

She laughs too, her back arching, her arms looping around me. "Want the recipe for another orgasm?"

"I believe that's what you're giving me."

The smile on her face is warm, vulnerable, then insanely dirty when it shifts into a grin of hungry, carnal bliss. "Here it is—more, more," she pants, her hands grappling at my back, tugging. They skate down to my ass, squeezing.

This woman.

She wants to feel.

She wants to feel me everywhere.

She wants a hard, powerful fucking—no teasing, no games. Just to be taken.

And I want her to have everything she longs for. I fuck her hard.

Deep.

Relentlessly.

Savoring, reveling in the sight of her losing her mind with lust. With desire.

As she arches against me, she begs for more, like she needs sex with me more than anything in the world, like she needs another orgasm more than oxygen.

And I don't want to deprive her.

I give her everything she wants, taking her over the edge again.

It is gorgeous and glorious to wring more than one climax from this woman. Under me, she looks spent and sated.

And I'm almost there too.

There's one thing I want.

But I don't have to ask for it. Because she pushes up to her elbows, drags soft fingers down my pecs, then reads my thoughts perfectly. "Want me to ride you? Finish you off like that?"

I groan so loud I bet they can hear me in the town square. A bolt of fresh lust slams into me. "You are indeed an angel. It's official."

In seconds, we switch positions, me flat on my back.

She straddles me, rises over my cock, then lowers herself back down. The grin on her face is filthy as she takes me in again, slides her palms up my chest, and presses them against me.

Then gives me the best view in the entire universe.

Her tits bouncing up and down as she rises up, slams down, then does it over and over, annihilating my senses until white-hot magic pulls me under as I come hard inside my next-door neighbor.

Who I should not be fucking.

Not at all.

But right now, I don't fucking care.

19

LIAM

That cut dinner short.

And I regret nothing.

The possibility of sex is why I picked an easy recipe. Why I came home an hour early and made it.

So it'd be ready.

Because when you invite a woman over for dinner, you shouldn't ignore her belly simply because you plan to enjoy her body for an appetizer.

Plus, I do like the possibility of dessert—her—and I'm hoping we get to have that course before Ethan returns in an hour and a half.

Ninety minutes.

I can do this.

I serve the pasta primavera, and we sit at the kitchen table.

"Speaking of recipes, did you follow one for this?" January digs her fork into the dish, waggles a piece of bow tie pasta on the tines, then pops it into her mouth, closing her luscious lips around the meal I made for her.

I smile, waggling my eyebrows. "I'm quite proud of myself for finding this recipe for your vegetarian heart and body. And one that doesn't have too many vegetables I despise in it." I take a bite of the pasta too.

She peers at the food. "So it's green veggies on your verboten list. But you're okay with . . . *gray* veggies?" She roots around on her plate, pointing to some of the mushrooms I picked up from the farmers market over the weekend.

What can I say? I was hopeful. Hopeful that I'd make dinner for her at some point, so I pregamed at the market.

"Mushrooms are good in my book."

She pokes an artichoke, spears it, then holds it up like she's captured it. "But artichokes? Aren't they green?"

"Ah. That is a most excellent question," I say, taking a bite, chewing, then answering her when I'm done. "I consider artichokes to be part of the so-called *beige* family of vegetables."

"I had no idea beige was a family of vegetables."

"Learn something new every day."

"You are a font of knowledge." She reaches for her glass of white wine and takes a healthy drink. When she sets down the glass, she picks up the fork again, pushes through the pasta, and lands on a slice of carrot. "And clearly orange vegetables are satisfactory, on account of *not* being green."

"Yes, they do seem to pass my general vegetable test."

She gestures to the salad she whipped up. The clever,

creative salad. "Good thing I didn't put Granny Smith apples or honeydew melons in there."

"Your salad is the height of brilliance."

With a naughty eyebrow arch, she blows on her fingernails. "Pretty proud of that one."

"As you should be, you temptress." My eyes shift to the absolutely delicious *fruit* salad she made. I tap my fork on the side of the bowl. "See? This is my idea of a perfect salad. Peaches. Pitted cherries. And raspberries. You are a genius."

Just to make my point, I dip my fork in, snag a peach, and savor every juicy bite of it.

She laughs. "You do like sweet things, Liam."

I arch one brow. "You're just figuring this out now?"

"I'm simply pointing it out now."

I lean in closer to her, my face inches away from hers. "I love sweet things. All sorts of sweet things. I enjoy all the sweetest tastes around." Because I can't resist how very sweet she is, I press a kiss to her cheek, sighing happily as I inhale her decadent scent. Maybe it's peaches—perhaps it's cherries. Whatever it is, her scent goes to my head.

She sets down her fork, shuddering the slightest bit. She slides a thumb across my jaw, then says, "How sweet am I?"

I bring my lips to hers, dusting a soft, barely-there kiss across them, murmuring, "The sweetest. You are absolutely the sweetest, January."

"Am I?" It comes out flirty.

I answer in kind, as I dust my lips along her neck, up to her ear, nipping that earlobe once more. "You taste and smell incredible. Your hair, your skin, your lips, and your absolutely delicious pussy that I would really like to kiss and lick and suck again tonight."

She hums in response, a sexy, sensual sound that makes me want to get down on my knees, slide my hands up her skirt, spread her legs, and devour her again.

Fanning her hand in front of her face, she stares at me, narrowing her pretty blue eyes. "You're trying to distract me from finishing all this delicious food you made for me. But I need it because I need my energy."

I'm all coy and playful as I say, "And what do you need your energy for?"

Her lips curve in a wicked grin. Her hand grips the hem of my shirt, tugging me a little closer. "I need it because it's almost eight and I'm going to want a little something for the road."

I groan my appreciation for her libido, for her mouth, for her mind. "Do you have any idea how sexy it is that you know exactly what you want?"

She gives a little shrug, her bare shoulder jutting up. "I want *you*. It's really quite simple."

That makes my heart squeeze. Maybe even glow. Warmth fans through me as I linger on her statement for a moment. This *thing* between us seems like it ought to be quite simple. Two adults enjoying each other's company.

But it's not simple at all.

It's fraught with complications.

Even though we want a lot of the same things— connection, intimacy, conversation—I'm keenly aware that we don't truly want the same things. I'm a relationship guy, and even if she's been a relationship woman before, that's not where she's at right now.

She's choosing to take a break.

She needs one.

Hell, she deserves it.

I can't push her. I won't push her. That's not my style, and it's also disrespectful of her journey. I can't imagine extracting myself from a long, loveless marriage, finding my own way, starting my own business, and then being sucked into the vortex of another relationship.

I wouldn't want that.

I understand why she doesn't either.

I move away from matters of the heart.

I need to zero in on something inanimate.

The furniture.

Perfect.

I gesture to the living room. "Thank you again for putting everything together. I know I said that when you first came over, but I was distracted by getting you naked, and now I want to properly thank you and say that was incredible, what you did."

"Oh, I think you did thank me properly," she says, playfully lingering on the words.

"I'm glad you feel it was a worthy way to show my gratitude."

"So worthy." She taps her chin. "But are you saying you're *not* distracted by getting me naked now?"

I shake my head, laughing. "I'm pretty much always

thinking about getting you naked. But I simply wanted to say your gift was a lovely, delightful surprise."

"Does it suit you? Your furniture?"

I glance at the newly built couch, chair, and table in the other room. "Yes. No. I don't know. I don't really care that much about furniture and whether it suits me."

With a thoughtful look on her face, she asks, "What do you care about?" She takes another bite of the pasta primavera as she waits for me to answer her latest question.

And this question is something I care deeply about.

Because this question is part of the connection between us, the easy way we can segue between teasing, dirty talking, and then diving in deep.

These talks matter to me.

I care about *her*.

About how we are together already.

But I don't say that yet. Now isn't the time. The time might not ever be.

Still, I answer honestly, repeating the question. "What do I care about?" I mull it over for a few seconds. "I care about doing the best job that I can as a vet. I care about helping animals. I care about my parents, my sisters, their children. I care the most, of course, about my own son, which still kind of amazes me every day, since I never intended to have a kid. And yet it's as if I can't remember a time when I didn't care for him."

She smiles, big and genuine. "Does it sometimes feel like the first seven years of his life didn't happen, because living as you know it started when he came into your life?"

My eyes widen, and I feel completely seen, thoroughly understood. "It does feel that way. And I loved my life beforehand. I thought it was great. Then he came into it, and suddenly it felt like the most important part of it had begun at last." I take a beat, noodling on those thoughts, on how right and true they feel. "Does that make any sense at all?"

After taking a drink of wine, she nods. "It makes perfect sense, because suddenly you know exactly what you're supposed to be doing and why. You go from sometimes wondering what the point of it all is to knowing what the point is of everything."

She's speaking my language and touching my heart. "Exactly. I never thought I'd enjoy being a father so much. I never even thought about it at all. Then it happened, and all I could think was *Wow, this must be why I really like being a vet.* I love taking care of small creatures, with four or two legs."

She brings her hand to her heart and swallows roughly, almost as if she's holding back tears. Then I'm certain she is, since her voice is wobbly as she says, "That is one of the sweetest things anybody has ever said."

I laugh, feeling the faintest flush in my cheeks, trying to dismiss the compliment. "Nah."

"Yes, Liam. It truly is."

I shrug, take another bite, chew, then set down my fork. "But that's just how it feels. And I look back on the fact that he was alive for nearly seven years and knocking about with his mother and doing all of these things in Florida, and I had no clue. I wish I had a telescope that would show me those times. I wish he could tell me stories about those days, because it feels like this black hole of his life that I will never know and never have access to," I say, the strength of my own wish powering my voice. I long for that insight into my son, and I'll never have it. "Maybe that's why I want every second now to be amazing. I want us to have a great relationship. To care about each other and look out for each other, because I didn't get to when he was younger."

She sets a hand on my arm, her palm soft and caring. "Do you regret that? That you missed all that time?"

"I do," I say heavily, a weight settling in my gut. "But it's stupid to regret it, since it was never in the cards."

"Did you ever want something with her? With Ethan's mom?"

"I didn't even think about it. It was truly a one-night stand. I met her at a bar in New York City, and we were safe. Used a condom. I didn't think twice about her or that night, to be honest. That's what I regret. I wish she'd been someone I wanted more with." I inhale deeply, then say something I don't share with anyone. I speak the truest regret. The one that hangs over me. "Mostly, I wish I'd had the chance for more. That she'd made other choices. That she'd given me the option to be his dad for longer. When he was born." I shake my head, annoyed all over again. "She didn't give me that opportunity for years, and when she finally did, I couldn't be angry with her. She was dying."

"But it's understandable that you wish things had been different."

"I would have been there for him. I would have shown up," I say, frustration welling inside me, but also sadness, since I never had that chance to be a father to an infant, a toddler, a four-year-old. "Now I simply wish that he could tell me stories about what he did when he was four."

I sound as wistful as I feel, and I try to stave off the melancholy, since this night isn't about regret. It's about coming together. But the soft, open look in January's eyes tells me it's okay to be frank about my feelings.

"It's like a blank slate in your past," she says gently.

"Yes, but on the other hand, I'm also used to looking at the world that way. When my patients come in with a pet they've adopted from a rescue, it's the same way. Sometimes they say things like *What do you think Fifi did for the first four months of her life? What did she do for the first year?* And I have no way of knowing, and just wonder. I make up stories, and they become part of the narrative for Fifi or Fido."

Taking another bite of the fruit salad, she's quiet as she eats. "So Ethan has his own narrative. He has a narrative that you'll never know, but maybe that's something the two of you can do someday. Maybe you can invent a story, sit down, and tell your own tale about what those seven years were like. And then you'll have a narrative you can share."

My heart thumps harder, pounding powerfully against my chest at that suggestion. It's both creative and touching. And something I'd love to do. "I love that idea, January. I think that's kind of beautiful. I could kiss you for that."

"Don't let me stop you."

I don't. I lean across the table, cup her cheek, and kiss the woman I care deeply for.

More than I intended to.

More than she has room in her life for.

But tell that to my heart.

It's speeding up, racing to be close to her, to this woman who's in a vastly different place than I am.

We are not the right-place, right-time couple.

We are out of alignment.

I find the will to break the kiss, take another bite of food, and enjoy the moment.

That's all this is, and that's okay. We can have this moment. Hell, maybe we can have a few moments—a few nights, even.

"I think that's one of the reasons you're so focused on family now. Because you're keenly aware of what you missed," she continues, seeing inside me, getting me.

"That's completely true. But that's not the only reason I'm focused on family."

She tilts her head, curiosity etching her features. "What's the other reason?"

I draw a breath. I haven't told her this yet. Odd because I sometimes feel like January and I talk about everything, but there is so much still to tell. "There's another reason I came back to town."

Her brow furrows. "There is? Oh, I can't believe I didn't ask. I assumed you came back to be near your parents. There's something else?"

I don't beat around the bush—I know that won't make it easier. "My dad is going blind." I explain about the condition he has and the pending surgery, looming quickly.

Her voice breaks once again. "I'm so sorry, Liam. How is he doing?"

"It's hard for him. But I think he's doing as well as he possibly can, and he has a lot of people here who love him."

She reaches for my hand. Squeezes it. "That includes you. That includes Ethan."

I turn my hand over, threading our fingers together, grateful for the contact. "It does. It definitely does."

"When did you find out?"

"About six months ago. That's when I started making plans to come back here."

"That's why family is so important to you. Not only because you're close to yours, but also because what's happening to your dad made you realize where you needed to be and what you wanted in life."

There's a weight to her words, almost as if she's underscoring that *this* is where I am in my life, and she's in a different spot. I want more. She does not.

We are all on our own paths, and rarely do those intersect with the paths of the ones we want.

My eyes travel over the gorgeous, kind, funny woman in my home, and land on her arms. Her sparrows. That seems like a safer topic than family—than the line that divides us.

I run a finger along the black birds painted on her skin. "Why'd you have these done?"

She draws a deep breath. "When I was feeling weighed down with Vince and my life, trying to figure out what I wanted, I hunted out images online that spoke to me. These jumped out. They felt like freedom. To make my own choices. To fly if I need to. To stay if I need to."

"You have that freedom. You always have that freedom. No one can take that away from you."

I can't fault that she wants different things than I do. If I had a fifteen-year-old, I don't know that I'd want to go back either. But I also don't want to talk about the things that stand between us. And so I slide back to the start of this conversation as I serve up another spoonful of the fruit salad. "So, you asked what I care about."

A grin spreads across her face. She likes this shift too. "Yes, tell me more."

I take a bite of a peach, moaning in pleasure. "Peaches. I care about peaches."

"Me too."

"I care about my bike, about taking care of my body, being fit, and yet still being able to eat ice cream. I care about my friends, about finding new friends here and keeping in touch with old friends in New York. I care about cookies and cake and brownies and sunshine and tea." I hold up a hand. "Correction: I care *deeply* about tea. I care about it so much that sometimes I think about marrying tea because I don't know how I'd wake up in the morning without it."

She points an accusing finger at me. "I thought you were a morning person. Now I learn you need tea?"

"I am a morning person powered by English breakfast."

"So if I came over some morning and stole all your

English breakfast tea, you wouldn't even make it out of bed?"

I slide a hand along her thigh, under her skirt. "You're not that cruel."

"You're right. I'm not. I'd never do that to you. Just like I hope you'd never steal my coffee."

We're so close our noses are nearly touching, and I have no choice but to kiss her again. When I break the kiss, I say, "I promise, January, I'll never take your coffee away."

She presses her palms together, as if her prayers have been answered. "Thank God. I can't live without it. I think it's something that happens when you turn thirty-five. You decide you want to marry things like aspirin and ibuprofen and coffee. I like being over thirty-five though."

"Same here. I feel like some of that craziness of my twenties has dwindled. Now, I can just kind of meet each day on its own terms," I say, finishing a cherry, then setting down my fork. "You learn to stop taking yourself so seriously, and then you learn to take the things seriously that ought to be taken that way. Like health and family, but not things like what kind of music you like or don't like. Time takes on a whole new quality when it no longer belongs solely to you. You learn to value it even more. Time becomes the thing that you'll do the most for. To make the best of it."

She's finished eating too, and I begin cleaning up, putting the plates in the sink. And then I ask, "And what about you? What do you care about?"

"I agree with you about time, for starters. And of

course I care about my daughter. I care about my friends. I care about being a kick-ass businesswoman. I care about doing an amazing job at work. I care about growing plants and veggies outside and giving back to the earth," she says, then takes a beat and moves behind me at the sink, her soft body pressed to mine. "I care about only sleeping with people I really like."

I did not expect that. That kind of came out of nowhere. But I love it, so much so that it heats my blood, warms my skin. I spin around. "I think that's my favorite thing on your list."

She dips her head, maybe a little shy. I tuck my finger under her chin. "Are you shy, January?"

She shakes her head. "I'm kind of aroused again."

My skin heats from her words. My cock hardens, and I can't resist touching her. I run my fingers along her arm, tracing them over her sparrows. "I like touching you. I love making you feel good. I like how you look and how you feel when you come."

"I like what you do to me," she whispers. "I like the way you feel under my hands. Your chest, your arms, your ass. You have a great ass, Liam. I love grabbing it when you're inside me."

Okay. Forget hard. My dick is an iron spike right now. "You're driving me crazy, woman. I am rock-hard here in the kitchen."

"And I'm wet," she whispers.

"You're fucking perfect," I say on a groan, my hands threading through her hair. "Now about that other orgasm . . ."

But she has something else in mind because she

slides down my body, gets on her knees, and unzips my jeans.

Before I can even think twice about giving her an O, she's got my dick in her mouth, and I have no interest in stopping her.

No interest whatsoever, since she's swirling her tongue around the head, licking me, sucking me, treating me like I'm an absolutely delicious piece of candy. Taking me deep, playing and gripping and stroking, as she lavishes delicious attention with her soft tongue and her firm lips and her gorgeous moans.

Soon I'm grunting and grabbing her hair, roping it around my fist, pulling and tugging and fucking into her mouth. "If you keep doing that, I'm going to come," I warn.

Ever so briefly, she pulls off, her lips against the head of my cock as she says, "That's the point." Then, in a heartbeat she's back on me, sucking me deep as pleasure roars through me.

Closing my eyes, I savor every second of coming in her throat. When she's done, I take her to the bedroom, and I have my dessert too until she comes on my lips.

I crawl up her body and murmur, "There's something I have to tell you."

"What is it?" Her eyes flicker with nerves.

I kiss her cheek, then pull back to meet her gaze. "I think I'm addicted to going down on you. I'm going to need to do it many more times."

Maybe this is my way of saying I want more.

That I want more than this night.

And as I say it, I don't think I ever felt like we could have only one time.

When she looks at me, wraps her arms around my neck, and says, "That's a really good addiction, and I'm happy to feed it," I'm pretty sure she never felt that way either.

Soon, I take her home, walking her to her door like a gentleman. I cup her cheek. "I'll see you soon."

She grabs my shirt, tugging on a fistful of fabric. "We're going to do that again, right?"

"Which part?" My heart soars, hoping, hoping, hoping for the same answer that I feel.

And she gives it to me. "Both."

I say yes.

20

JANUARY

When I have breakfast with my daughter before she goes to school the next morning, I look her in the eyes over the scrambled eggs, toast, and peaches. She takes a bite, chewing, and I do the same, then I set down my fork, my chest swelling with a clobbering wave of affection for her.

That's not necessarily a surprise.

I constantly feel affection for her. But when it's your normal state of heart, you don't always notice it. This time, though, the wave crashes over me. And I know why.

"I'm lucky," I say.

She shoots me a curious look. "Why are you lucky?"

My heart thumps harder, filling up like a hot-air balloon with love for this kid. "Because I've had you your whole life."

I get what's coming to me. A flummoxed *what on earth are you talking about* look. It's paired with the waggle of one eyebrow. Then a lift of the other one. "You feeling okay there, Mom?"

I nod, my throat tightening. I reach for my coffee, take a hit of the life-sustaining beverage, and try to speak past the knot. "I'm lucky because I've known you since you were born."

"Well, duh. You gave birth to me. Of course you've known me since I was born. That's kind of what being a mom is." She snags another piece of egg.

"But some parents don't get to know their kids their whole life."

A solemn look crosses her eyes. "Is this going to be a sad conversation where you tell me that you're sick or that someone has died?"

"No, God no." I reach for her shoulder, squeezing, then squash the notion that seemed to bring such fear to her voice immediately. "I just mean some parents don't know for a while that they've had kids."

She breathes a sigh of relief, but then her brow pinches in confusion again. "What do you mean?"

"It happens." And since Liam's story of fatherhood isn't a secret, I say, "That's the case with Liam and Ethan. Liam didn't even know he had a son until Ethan was more than six years old, and his mom brought Ethan to him because she had cancer."

Her eyes glisten. "Oh, that's so sad. And hard. That sounds really hard for everyone. And weird too. I'm sorry about his mom."

"Me too. But it also made me realize something. I'm so glad I've known you your whole life." My voice trembles. "I'm glad I didn't miss any of it."

My daughter smiles at me in the most genuine, wonderful way. In a way that hooks into my chest, that knocks the air from my lungs. That makes me realize that your heart truly does beat outside your body when you have a child. That all your emotions are both stored in the container of your heart and spill over it at the exact same time.

"But I don't remember that much from when I was younger," Wednesday adds, tilting her head and screwing up the corner of her lips, lost in thought. "But I think I was happy. I've always been happy, right?"

My smile stretches to the edges of the world. I run a hand down her soft hair. "That's another reason why I'm lucky. You've always been a pretty happy kid."

"I don't think it's just luck. I mean, look, I like you," she says, like it's no big deal, when it's the biggest deal. "You're cool. You're a good mom. That's why I'm happy. And Dad is a good dad, even though I don't see him much. I talk to him a lot. We text all the time. And he was a good dad when he was here."

The lump in my throat expands to the size of a golf ball. "Vince is a very good dad."

She takes another bite of her eggs, then a drink of her coffee, since she's already on the sauce. "Even when you and Dad weren't really crazy about each other, I was still mostly happy, I guess, because you guys were never jerks to each other. Some of my friends who have divorced parents—their parents can be jerks. Yelling at each other, treating each other badly. But you and Dad were never like that. You were just two people who weren't really right for each other."

It is amazing how much a child can see.

We think we can fool them. We think, as parents, by spelling words out loud before they can read, by whispering, by slapping on false smiles, that we can shield them from the truth. But children are always so much more astute than we think. That's why I've never wanted to fool my daughter. I've always tried to be open and honest with her because that's how I want her to be with me. "No, we really weren't right for each other."

She picks up her plate and walks over to the sink. "Is this your way of telling me you're right for Liam?"

I blanch, whipping my head around to look at her as she sets down her dish. "What are you talking about?"

She rolls her eyes, an even bigger eye roll this time, as she returns to the table, grabs my plate, and takes it to the sink too, rinsing both. "Mom. Do you think I don't know what you did last night?"

I sputter, a cartoon character running in place in midair. "You know?"

"Aww." She gives me a sarcastic look that works particularly well coming from a fifteen-year-old. "It's so cute how you don't deny it. Also, I don't want any details, but it's so obvious that you're hot for him."

I slap my hands over my ears. "Oh my God, please stop."

She points at me, laughing. "No, you stop."

I lower my hands. "Also, please know this is not my way of telling you that we're seeing each other."

"But you are seeing him?"

Am I? I don't know how to answer that, so I say nothing.

She's undeterred. "Look, here's the deal. He seems like a cool guy, and Ethan's kind of cool too. I mean, for, like, an almost ten-year-old. His birthday is soon, so we need to get him a card or a prezzie."

"We do. We'll go shopping soon."

"And maybe we can get that cat soon too?" she asks, waggling her brows.

"The cat?"

She rolls her eyes. "Ripley."

I snap my fingers. Of course. The Ripley plan. "Fine, we'll look for Ripley soon."

"Soon, as in this month or this decade?"

"This month," I say, laughing.

She gives me a thumbs-up. "I'm holding you to it. Also, just go date Ethan's dad, okay?"

"You're hilarious. I wasn't asking permission to date him."

She yanks her head back, going full reality show *oh no you didn't*. "Well, you should ask permission to date him, girl."

I laugh. "Is that how it goes now? I have to ask permission to date someone?" I move over to the sink and load the plates into the dishwasher.

"You haven't seen anyone since Dad. You haven't even gone on a single date," she says, once more proving my point. Kids don't miss much. They are sponges. They absorb all we say and do. "These things don't get past me. I have eyes and ears."

"I made you that way. Eyes and ears," I say, since sometimes teasing is easier.

Grabbing the elastic on her wrist, she loops her hair into a low pony. "I'm just saying, I know you haven't been with anyone. So this is kind of a big deal. And I know that you guys like each other."

When she says that, my stomach flips. A brand-new smile spreads across my face. My eyes, I'm sure, are lit with sparklers.

She points at me with wicked glee. "Look at you. Just look at you. You're so pathetic, it's adorable. Just go out with him."

And I answer the question I didn't earlier. "I kind of am seeing him, but it's not that simple, sweetie. We want different things. That makes it hard. He wants a bigger family."

She cringes. "More kids?"

I nod. "Yeah, and I feel like I'm on the homestretch. It wasn't easy being pregnant at twenty-one. But I did it. I made it work. I made *us* work."

"You did make us work. A baby would be . . ." Her nose wrinkles. "Weird?"

"Kind of weird," I second.

Her lips purse, and she swallows harshly, like she's the one with the grapefruit in her throat. "But there's no reason you shouldn't just enjoy it in the meantime, then." She pastes on a grin. She sets a hand on my shoulder, looks me in the eye, and says, "I'm glad I've known you my whole life."

I have no choice. I crush her in a hug and tell her I love her a million times until she heads to school.

I wave goodbye.

I don't think I was looking for permission from my daughter. I definitely don't feel like I needed it.

But sometimes that's what kids do. They give you their permission anyway.

I'll take it. I'll definitely take it.

21

JANUARY

That's what we do.

We see each other.

Every day.

On the one hand, it's because we're neighbors.

On the other, it's because we're dopey, happy, smiley new lovers.

In the mornings, as Wednesday heads to school and Liam and Ethan hop on their bikes, I give him a grin that says both *We are cats who ate the canaries* and *I like you so very much.* He flashes a smile back at me that says *I'm happy to see you* and also, *I want to see you naked.*

So much is said in our silent stares, but nothing is hidden because our feelings are written in our eyes and expressions.

In the evenings, we find ways to spend time together.

Sitting on the porch swing and talking while eating ice cream.

Popping over for a late-night rendezvous.

He helps Wednesday with a science assignment.

I help Liam fix his dryer.

A week after our first night together, once Ethan goes to bed and Wednesday does the same, I do that thing that makes me feel like a teenager. I slip next door to see the cute guy who lives there. We giggle as we head to his bedroom, but that still doesn't feel like enough distance from the other rooms, so we duck into the master bathroom.

He lifts me onto the marble vanity, wedges himself between my legs, and then stares at me, heat in his brown eyes. There's desire there, and endless affection in his words when he says, "I thought about you all day."

"You're just trying to get under my skirt again," I tease.

"Oh yes, I am absolutely dying to get under your skirt, but I also thought about you. I thought about fucking you. I thought about the way you smiled at me this morning. I thought about having dinner with you again. I thought about all those things."

My heart does a wild loop the loop. "I like seeing you," I confess, and it feels good to get it off my chest.

"You enjoy meeting me like this in my bathroom?"

"I do. I kind of like meeting you anywhere," I say, amazed that it's so easy to speak the truth to him. It's so simple to be honest about all these burgeoning feelings.

I don't know why. Maybe because we both know the score? We both know I'm not his Ms. Right.

But I *am* his Ms. Right Now.

He ducks his head against my neck, burying his face there, pressing his lips to my skin, traveling up to my ear, and giving me a kiss that makes me tremble all over. "I want to do all those things with you. I want to have dinner with you and take you out and walk around town, but right now I really want to be inside you again."

"I want the exact same thing."

I wrap my legs around him, tugging his pelvis against me, sliding my hands around his neck and bringing him close. I kiss him hard and hungrily. He glances down at my dress and runs a thumb over the fabric of my skirt. "You've taken to wearing sundresses around me."

"I'm a fast learner."

"You are indeed," he says, sliding open a drawer and reaching for a condom.

He kisses me, deeply and thoroughly, with so much passion that I am panting and gasping. I'm sure he can tell that it won't take me long.

Breaking the kiss, he slides off my panties, and I push down his workout shorts, his boxers too. I run a hand along his thick, hot length, savoring the velvet-smooth feel of his skin, how his eyes close, and then squeeze shut. Then the small groans he makes, the noises that rumble from him as I stroke.

But not for long.

On a sexy, needy moan, he stops my hand, opens the condom, and rolls it on. He brings himself between my legs, teasing against my wetness. I set my palms behind me on the bathroom counter, bracing myself on them, angling my back so my breasts push up, and giving him the perfect angle to fuck me hard and deep.

In seconds, he's all the way in me, and I am lost. I am lost in the sensations that whip through me. And the connection that I feel with him already.

And as he fucks me harder, the way I like it, because he's already learned how I like it, everything feels like it's happening so soon.

But it also doesn't feel soon at all.

Because I remember all we said that first night. *From the second I met you, I wanted to kiss you.*

And that's attraction, that's connection.

But the wanting intensified before we touched, grew stronger as I got to know him, and it combusted the night we came together.

It's fire now.

It's become *this*. The way we fit. The way I wrap my arms around his neck, bring him close, and kiss the hell out of him as he thrusts inside me. And it's *this* too, him whispering in my ear, "God, you feel so fucking good, love."

Love.

It's simply a British term of endearment. It doesn't mean anything more than *honey* or *goddess* or *babe*. But I love that it came out of his mouth only in the heat of the moment. That he's not the type of man who throws *love* around with abandon.

It's almost like a sweet, dirty foreign language, reserved for me. And I use it with him too, in my own way, telling him, "I love when you fuck me, Liam."

"Yeah? You like it when I'm deep in you? When I take you hard?" He brings a hand between my legs, stroking my clit, rubbing me right where I want him. Pleasure twists in my belly, blooms, then radiates through my whole body as I dig my nails into his back, wrap my legs tight around him, and groan, "I'm coming."

"Come with me, love."

There it is again. *That word.*

We could become so much more than sex.

But maybe we already are.

* * *

That Friday afternoon, he gets off work early.

I do too, and I wait on the edge of town by the train tracks. The sun is high above my head as I rest my hand above my eyes, watching for him. A gorgeous man walks toward me. If I thought my heart thundered before, it does even crazier things now. It's like a drum beating loudly in my chest, jackhammering in my ears. When he sees me, he comes right up to me, cups my cheek, and kisses me.

We wander along the train tracks like two lovers in a movie, walking into the afternoon sun as we talk about the town, the women, my friends, our businesses.

It feels like this could be ours.

That we could have these walks, these talks, these kisses.

That's the trouble. Everything feels so possible with him.

22

LIAM

The thing about new relationships is that when they're good, they're so, so good.

And infatuation—it does this thing to you.

It scrambles your brain, works its way around your heart, and makes it so all you want is to see the other person.

I start something I never did much in New York.

I take lunch breaks.

I have a little more free time here, but I also have the red-blooded motivation to step away.

The first week we're together, we grab all the time we can. Sometimes January swings by, picks me up in her truck, and we drive. We go to the train tracks, and we sit and make out in the front seat. Then we talk. We talk about growing up in Duck Falls and Lucky Falls.

We talk about college, about our twenties and thirties, about New York and California, San Francisco and the town in Surrey where I lived before becoming an American citizen.

That makes her laugh—that I'm a citizen.

"Why is that funny?"

"Because you still have your accent, so you seem British to me."

"Do you want me to get rid of it?" I joke.

"God, no."

"You only want me for my accent."

Shrugging, she slides a hand up my shirt. "It *is* a nice feature."

"Then it's a good thing I kept it," I whisper. "All the better to seduce you with."

I learn about some of her favorite books, and how she has a thing for women's fiction. She eats up stories about modern women living their lives, facing challenges. I tell her about the science articles I like to read and the books I listen to that keep my brain fresh. We talk about the world and what we want for it. We chat about how we love when the trees are green, the air is clear, and it feels like Mother Earth is exhaling peacefully.

Sometimes we drive past the wineries, admiring the rolling hills, January's hand wrapped in mine as we talk more. I'll tell her about a patient that came in, and she'll tell me about a client on a project she's working on, how she's kicking ass and beating Big Beams Construction like the badass businesswoman she is. And then I'll tell her a story about Ethan and something funny that happened at school, and she'll share one about Wednesday.

I learn more about Alva and Missy, and I tell her about Oliver, Summer, and Aunt Jane.

It all feels so good. But it also feels like it could be too good to be true.

I try to let myself just enjoy it. To give in to whatever magic is happening, to the moment, to all of these moments that are winding together. Only I can't help but worry about when they are going to unravel and how much it'll hurt when they do.

But it doesn't always hurt. Sometimes it just feels good.

It's Friday again, and I have two hours free in the middle of the day, and she does too. At her house, we have lunch, and then we make love in her bed as the sun streams in through the window. This time we don't use a condom because we're both safe and we're both clean, and it feels absolutely incredible to pull her on top of me, to slide my hands up her body, to feel her taking me with no barriers.

Her hair fans around my face as her gorgeous body swivels, sways, moves up and down my length. Her lips fall to mine, and she tries to kiss me, she tries so damn hard, but soon she becomes lost in the pleasure.

The kisses turn sloppy. They become groans and moans and pants. Then they turn into whispers and words like . . .

Feels so good.

Never been better.

Love this.

We're coming together and falling apart.

After, as we lie next to each other, naked and hot and tangled on the bed, I run a hand down her side. "This seems like it's been more than just a few times."

"It does."

"At the risk of stating the patently obvious, I like you so much."

Her grin is magic, and she says, "To state the obvious, I like you so much too."

That's what makes this tryst so wonderful and so dangerous. We are falling into something that can't possibly last.

23

———

JANUARY

I'm outside tending to the garden when Ethan and Liam return from school on their bikes. My heart thumps at the sight of them wheeling down the street. Liam's eyes lock with mine from the bike. Ethan stops and says hi, then declares, "I have to go play baseball right now."

Liam shrugs. "It's true. He does *have* to."

Ethan rolls to the driveway, and Liam calls out to him, "Why don't you just go inside and clean up and set your backpack down?"

"Then can we go to the park?" Ethan looks at me and asks, "Want to come with us, January?"

I smile, glancing at Liam, who mouths, *Only if you want to.*

"I'd love to."

Ethan runs inside as Liam asks, "What are you doing tonight? After you've played baseball?"

"Do you want me to sneak up on the roof?"

"Let's get a blanket and lie there and stare at the stars."

"You have to stop saying these things."

"What? Thoroughly romantic things that make you fall for me?"

My chest flips. Is it that obvious I'm falling for him? Am I trying to hide it? No, I'm not. "Yes, those things."

"Actually, why don't we sit outside by the pool after he goes to bed?"

"So we don't roll off the roof while making out?"

"Exactly."

"Beauty and brains. How can I resist the hot British vet next door?"

"I don't think you can," he says, all deadpan and then some.

After Wednesday and I join them for a casual baseball game, running the bases, striking out, hitting pop flies and the occasional dinger, we debate the greatest ballplayers of all time.

I say Sandy Koufax.

Ethan says Steve Trout.

Wednesday says he's wrong.

We all laugh, and on the way home, we run into Ethan's new friend Travis and his two dads. Ethan makes plans with Travis to play baseball that weekend, and I catch up with his parents, who run the local hardware shop.

"We've got some new power tools you'll like," David says, his blue eyes glinting with delight.

"Don't you just know the way to a lady's heart," I say with a wink.

David's husband, Rob, wraps an arm around him.

"Yes. Either power tools or a dress with pockets as my friend Jackson always says," he says.

I poke Liam. "Take notes. Dresses with pockets, and drills."

Liam taps his temple. "It's all been filed away."

We say goodbye and continue on our way. The four of us—Liam, Wednesday, Ethan, and me—chat about dogs versus cats, pizza versus cake, and whether Wednesday could hack into the Dodgers roster and list Ethan as a pinch hitter one night.

She says she could.

Ethan doubts her.

She gives him a noogie.

He squirms away, cackling.

Liam and I just smile and laugh, holding hands, and it feels a little bit like magic.

When we reach our homes, we disperse, and after dinner with my daughter and time spent reviewing her English essay and finishing some invoicing, I say good night to her.

She gets in bed with a book and a pointed stare. "I know what you're doing."

I just shrug and say, "What?"

"I know you're going over there to see him. I know you're doing that every night."

"Do you want me to deny it?"

She laughs. "You couldn't deny it if you tried. It's so obvious from the googly-eyed way you do everything these days."

"Am I googly-eyed?"

"You are so googly-eyed."

"Good night, Spawn."

As I leave her room, I send a note to Alva.

January: Am I googly-eyed?

Alva: Over the guy next door that you're falling madly for?

January: Yes.

Alva: I'm cackling so hard right now I'm actually screaming.

January: Are you serious?

Alva: Can't you hear me?

January: Am I that transparent?

Alva: I can read you. Also, stop analyzing everything. Go live your life. Go be googly-eyed for your neighbor. You deserve it.

I don't know that anyone deserves anything, but I know this—I'm taking my happiness. As I leave my house, shutting the door behind me, I catch a glimpse of the sparrows on my arms.

I have the strangest realization. Heading over to see

Liam feels like freedom. It feels like me chasing my freedom. I don't know what to make of that feeling. I simply know that it *is*.

I join him in the backyard on the chaise lounge by the pool, snuggling next to him as he wraps an arm around me. We stare up at the September sky, and he points to the constellations. "This is the cheesy scene in a movie where I tell you that's Cassiopeia, and then I say something like *You're prettier than Cassiopeia.*"

I swat at him. "One, you're making fun of all romantic movies. Two, you're making fun of me."

"Yes, I am doing all of that, and I am delighting in it."

"You're evil."

He presses a kiss to my shoulder. "I am. Yet you're still here. You like my evil side."

"How can you take a wildly romantic moment and turn it into a mockery?"

He arches a brow. "One of my many talents?"

"You have a lot of talents."

We let the teasing fade as we snuggle together. As he presses a kiss to my cheek, he whispers, "It is nice being romantic with you."

I move closer. "You're prettier than Cassiopeia."

He laughs, and I do too, then we're quiet.

Wishes shift inside me, making room for new wants and desires. Still, I don't know how to move past this huge roadblock.

He wants a bigger family. I don't.

I don't want to start over in the family-making department, but I don't want to lose him either.

Just focus on the here and now.

"Tell me what you did today," I say, trying to root myself to the moment.

"I saved a dog's life," he says. He tells me about a dog who was hit by a car and brought in immediately, and how he devoted all his focus and energy to saving the poor pup and now the pooch is doing better.

My heart, my God, it melts to pieces.

"That's amazing," I choke out.

"I'm glad I was there."

That's all he says about it. I reach my hand up, stroking his hair. He closes his eyes and relaxes a little bit as I touch him.

"Are you going to get a dog still?" I ask.

With his eyes closed, he whispers, "Yes. Are you going to get a cat?"

"I hope so," I say. "Do you like Jason Segel movies?"

He opens his eyes and laughs at me. "That's a non sequitur. Jason Segel?"

"*I Love You, Man* and *Forgetting Sarah Marshall* and *The Muppets*. I think he's really funny."

His lips curl up in a grin. "Why are you asking me if I like Jason Segel movies?"

"Because I do. I like him."

"And do you want me to have the same taste as you?"

"I just want to know what your taste is."

He brings his face closer, brushes his lips across mine, and whispers, "I love Will Ferrell like crazy."

It sounds like he's talking about Will Ferrell, but *not* about Will Ferrell at the exact same time. When we kiss, I'm positive neither one of us is thinking about Will Ferrell or Jason Segel at all.

As Liam's hands skate up my body and mine slide under his shirt, I'm aware of a brand-new desperation at the thought of losing him.

Because I might not be able to figure us out.

But right now, I'm getting lost in pleasure, getting lost in sensation as he touches me, making me want him even more.

I can tell where this night is going. To the bedroom. Before we venture there, I touch his face, stroke a thumb along his cheek, and meet his gaze. "What am I going to do about this?" I ask, feeling brave.

Wildly, incredibly brave.

"About what?"

"About you," I whisper.

"What do you want to do about me?"

"I don't know what to do about the fact that I'm falling so hard for you, Liam."

He tries but fails to contain a grin. "What am I supposed to do about the fact that I'm falling for you?"

We don't have any good answers. So we answer it in a way that we're both quite good at.

"Let's go inside," I say.

In his room, I take off my clothes. He climbs over me, grabs my wrists, pins them over my head, and sinks inside me.

We're quiet tonight. Thoroughly, completely quiet, saying nothing, only murmuring under our breaths.

I'm quiet for one reason.

I'm afraid that if I speak, I'll tell him that I might, just might, be willing to change everything for him.

24

LIAM

My mother is tense and worried the whole time my father's in the operating room. I take the day off for this latest surgery, distracting her by playing Words with Friends on our phones, and that settles her down until we get the good news that all is well.

We take him home, and he rests most of the day.

When he wakes up, he jokes and says, "I can see again. I can see again."

I don't want to laugh, but I do anyway. It makes him happy, and we all know he can't see that well, not like he used to. Still, the procedure should help lengthen the time until he loses his vision fully.

After spending the afternoon with him at their house, I give him a kiss on the forehead. "I'll be back tomorrow."

I keep my word, stopping by after work with Ethan, who reads his grandfather some Percy Jackson, then he says he has to go play with Galinda and Elphaba.

"Did you pick a cake for your birthday?" my dad calls out.

"Yes! I want every flavor imaginable. Vanilla, chocolate, coconut, and caramel," Ethan says.

"That's only four."

"I'll take anything else you want to get too. I'm easy like that." Then he races out to the backyard, flops down onto the grass, and lets the dogs lick his face.

As I stare at my son from the kitchen window, a barrage of questions flies through my mind. I know he's always loved dogs, baseball, and the water.

I know he liked sweets when he was younger too.

But what did his mom leave out on her list of instructions? What if something changed? Like I said to January, I'll never know.

I'll never have the keys to the age-zero-to-seven years.

As I watch him, though, I remember what January said the first night we slept together—write our own narrative.

Make up a new story.

Invent something fresh.

I draw a deep breath, imagining the years I missed.

And trying, trying so hard, to let them go.

* * *

Later that night, after I've put Ethan to bed, Kerri rings. "So, how's that money tree working out in your backyard?"

"Oh, it's fantastic. I just go out and shake it all the time."

"You know, everybody hates you."

I laugh as I sink down on the new couch, the one January assembled. I slide my hand along the cushions as I talk, thinking of her. "You hate me because I didn't actually have to use a dating app?"

"Yes. We hate you because of that."

"Who is *we* exactly?"

"All women who don't get to pluck men off trees in the yard. I speak for them."

"But you're happily married," I say, my brow knitting.

"I still hate you for it. Now tell me all about her. I'm dying to know the details of the woman who's captured your affections," she says.

I grin, all too eager to tell her. "She's wonderful and fantastic. Smart and kind. Funny and sarcastic, and she has the hugest heart."

Kerri sighs happily. "Am I meeting her at Ethan's party this weekend?"

"I hope so. I'll ask her to be there."

"Excellent. Dare I say it?"

"Say what?"

"She sounds like *the one*."

My heart pinches, a sharp pang winging through me. "She does sound like it, but I don't think she wants that, Ker."

"She doesn't want to walk down the aisle and pop out babies with you?" she asks, more serious now.

"I don't think she does." I frown, wishing things were different.

"Oh." My sister is quiet for a long beat. "I mean, every woman should make her own choice, and good for her and all. But how is that going to gel with what you want?"

Scrubbing a hand across my jaw, I shrug, my whole body weighing a thousand pounds. "Don't know."

She allows a comforting silence to pass, then says, "I hope she changes her mind. For your sake."

I sigh, not sure what to say.

"Or that you change yours."

But change it about what? That's the thing—I don't know. I came to California so certain about what I wanted, and now I feel lost, like I'm wandering through the woods without a map.

Like I'm in IKEA without January.

After we say goodbye, a text from Oliver flashes on my screen, asking if life in California is perfect.

I write back, sort of lying, sort of telling the truth.

Liam: It's fantastic.

He sees through me immediately.

Oliver: That means you're getting your knob wet.

. . .

I have a laugh at his crude turn of phrase but expect nothing different from my cousin—in a good way.

Liam: Is that the only reason a man can be happy?

Oliver: No, but it certainly helps. So, is it the fox who assembled your furniture while you were at work?

Liam: Yes. I've been seeing her a lot.

Oliver: So, it looks like you found Ms. Right. Good on you.

But that's not the case at all. My shoulders slump, impossibly heavy, heavier, even, than when I was speaking to Kerri. The truth seems even starker now as I share it with Oliver.

Liam: That's the trouble. She's not interested in that.

Oliver: Oh. Can't you convince her? Have you lost your touch, coz? Are you no longer convincing?

But what do I really need to convince her of? To be serious? To be a partner? To want more, so much more?

And if you can convince someone, is that person agreeing to have a family just for you? Is it fair to even ask that of someone?

Why can't it be easy, finding the right person at the right time?

But it's not, and asking for what you want is harder than fixing a dog's leg.

I wince as I imagine trying to say those awkward words to January. *Want to be mine all the time, build a life together and maybe, just maybe, a family?*

Trying to string together the words to convey my desires ties me in knots.

Knots I never quite expected.

But . . . what are my desires?

Are they still the same?

Because as I lie here, staring at the ceiling, wondering about my future, the next few months, the next few years look muddled.

For the first time in ages, I'm not even sure of what I want.

And I don't know how to turn the glass half full.

All else aside, the first thing I need to convince January of is coming to Ethan's birthday party. When I see her the next morning on the sidewalk, I ask, "Would you like to come to Ethan's birthday party this weekend?"

"I'd love to. And I was going to be seriously pissed if you didn't invite me."

A grin takes over my whole face, and I feel certain of

this much—of her, of how much I like spending time with her. "Oh, have you been tracking his birthday?"

"He's only told me twenty times that it's this weekend. I've already bought him a gift."

"You know the way to his heart."

"Well, I am raising a child. They do like gifts."

"I like gifts," I say, and I tug at the waistband of her shorts.

She rolls her eyes. "You like the gift of getting in my pants."

"It's the gift that keeps on giving. Can you blame me? It's a wonderful present."

She runs her fingertip down my nose. "And so is being asked to your son's party."

I'm aware of what I'm asking her. I'm asking her to meet my parents. And it feels terrifying.

But also . . . not terrifying at all.

Maybe when I'm there, surrounded by family, I'll know exactly what I want.

* * *

That Saturday, we head over to Lucky Falls in her pink truck. Of course, Wednesday was invited, but she had a pressing fifteen-year-old engagement to attend to—something about melting marshmallows with Audrey for their YouTube channel.

Inside my parents' place, I introduce January to my father, who shakes her hand and says, "I hear you're gorgeous and brilliant."

They chat for a bit about the town, then her business, then a job she just finished, and it's lovely how easily they're getting along.

A few minutes later, my mum pulls us aside and says to January, "So you're the neighbor."

"I am."

"Great. I want to show you these cupboards that need a little bit of work, but I insist on paying you." She beckons January into the kitchen.

January shakes her head. "I insist on you not paying me."

"No, I must. It's just how it is."

That's my mum, already diving into things, enlisting January in her life and doing it on her terms.

"You will not give me any money, Mrs. Harris."

From across the room, I call out, "Mum, you're not going to win this one."

She tuts, shakes a finger at me, then says, "Oh, yes, I am."

January flashes me a smile. "She's not going to win this one."

My father chuckles and says, "Love, I don't think you're going to win this one."

I sit down next to my dad as January heads inside with my mum to check out the cupboards, and he nods in their direction. "What are you going to do? Do you know?"

I let out a long breath. What am I going to do? That's exactly what I have to figure out.

As in, what the fuck am I going to do because I'm in love with a woman who doesn't want what I want at all?

I don't know. I don't know. And I don't know.

Do I just let go of everything I thought I wanted?

Say goodbye to my dreams?

Let them fall to the ground and melt like snow when it touches concrete?

"I have no idea," I say.

"Maybe you need some time to think about what you want."

Time.

That sounds wise.

But can I sort it out when I'm tugging her into my bedroom every night, making love to her, whispering sweet nothings, and falling mercilessly in love?

Ethan stays behind at my parents' house for the night.

On the ride home, January must sense that my mind is far away. Once we pull into my driveway, she runs a hand through my hair, her eyes concerned. "What's going on?"

That's the issue.

I'm used to knowing what I want.

Used to understanding my heart.

Accustomed to making decisions.

And I don't know a damn thing anymore.

The more I'm near her, the harder it is to understand what I want and what I'll regret.

There's no point mincing words. I turn, meet her gaze, and speak the truth. "I think I need a few days to figure out what's going on with us."

She blinks. Parts her lips. Gulps. When she speaks, it's in a strangled voice. "A break? You need a break?"

I cup her cheek, sadness flooding my entire being.

But I need time.

I need to know what to do, how to change, *what* to change. "I do. I do need it because I want all of these things and you don't, and I can't keep falling in love with you if you don't want the same things I do."

There it is.

I've told her that I'm in love with her.

She swallows roughly, licks her lips, then says, "A time-out is a good idea, then, because I'm in love with you too."

25

JANUARY

The next morning, Betty waves me over as I'm outside checking on my flowers.

"January," she says, beckoning as she waters her garden. It isn't drowning this time. I head over to her house, stopping at the white fence.

She waggles her eyebrows, her slate-blue eyes twinkling with mischief. "Inquiring minds want to know. Is his tush just as biteable as it looks from a distance?"

I shake my head, frowning, unable to joke about biteable olives with our *break status* tugging me down. "You're not going to get that out of me."

She tuts. "Please, do an old woman a solid."

"You're not old. You're . . . what? Sixty-two?" I ask, hoping to divert her attention away from Liam and me, especially since I don't think there is a Liam and me anymore. I don't know how to cross our impasse, and it's breaking my heart.

"Please. I am sixty-one. Don't age me up." She moves the hose over her peonies, drizzling a little bit of water on them before she sets it down on the lawn, heads to the faucet, turns it off, then joins me again. "I had my daughters young. Just like you with Wednesday. And we're close too."

"That is true." Missy often tells me how well she gets along with her mom, since they're only twenty-three years apart.

Betty wags a finger at me. "But I want to know about the olive scale."

I don't want to go there, so I sidestep. "Your lawn looks great."

She narrows her eyes. "Are you having trouble in paradise? Missy and I were glad that you were the one who got him."

But does that matter if I can't keep him? "I'm not sure it'll last."

She gives me a look of utter disbelief. "How could it not last? You can fix anything in the house, and he can take care of all your pets. You're both hot to trot for each other. What problems could you possibly have?"

Problems like life goals.

Like wants.

Like the future.

I give an easy shrug. "Who knows?" I try to keep it light and breezy. This isn't the time or the place to break it all down.

"Oh," she says, as if the light bulb has flicked on. Like she's figured it all out. "Kids. You want more and he doesn't?"

I let out a long breath, wishing she hadn't nailed it in reverse, but weirdly glad that I have an outlet. "More like the other way around. But I think maybe I should change my mind."

"Ah," she says with a sage nod. "You thought you were done, but now you aren't sure?"

I didn't intend to have this conversation with my neighbor, but sometimes it's easier to voice deep truths to someone who's *not* regularly in your life. Who only appears in it tangentially. Saying these words to Betty helps me understand them. Helps them take shape.

"I'm thirty-seven. It's not that I'm too old to have kids. I might be able to, but I also don't know . . . and there is so much to consider." I take a beat, collecting my thoughts. "And yet he's kind of amazing."

"But you have a career to think about now too," she points out, drawing up her shoulders like she's calling on all her woman strength. "You've started building your business. I had my girls when I was young, and by the time I was forty-one, they were out of the house and I was able to start my flower shop. That had been my dream, something I'd always wanted to do. Would I have been able to do that if I'd had another baby? Who knows? There are all sorts of things to think about. But I'm glad I opened my shop and glad I had something of my own."

"Glad, too, that you didn't have to bring a baby with you to the store?"

She flashes a sympathetic smile. "Yes, dear. That too."

What would it be like to have a baby again? How would I get any work done? Would I take the baby to jobs? Get a nanny? Would Liam stay home? The practical stuff is so daunting and terrifying.

But it's worth considering because he wants it.

I try to picture what it'd be like to be pregnant again.

Would he want to start right away? What if we wanted to be together just as a couple for a few years? Then I might not be able to get pregnant. Would he resent me if I couldn't?

I don't share all of this with Betty. It's too personal. I don't have the answers to any of these questions.

But then, an adorable towhead toddles from inside the house onto the front porch, stretches, and says, "Nana, I woke up from my nap. Can we draw?"

Betty turns around, her smile lighting up her features. "Of course, sweetheart. Anything you want, my little lovebug."

As Betty walks over to the porch, I can't resist. I join her. When she picks up her little granddaughter and brings her close, nuzzling her hair, I get that feeling in my chest, the one I get when I'm holding a baby.

A feeling a lot of women get. That feeling of wanting them.

Betty must see it in my eyes because she turns to me and says, "Nora's a sweetheart. Do you want to give her a little hug?"

Nora reaches her hands out, and I take her in my arms, close my eyes, and inhale that fresh, sweet smell.

Could I truly do this?

Not for him. But for me.

That's the question.

And I need to find the answer.

26

LIAM

My first patient on Monday is none other than the devil himself.

Saul.

But Maya doesn't seem as frazzled or as manic as she did on our date, or on her first visit to the clinic *after* our date. She made an appointment a few weeks ago and has been working through her cat's issues.

She's calmer, more hopeful, and Saul seems to be doing better too.

"I've been able to leave the house a few times without him. I was able to go to the library," she says with obvious enthusiasm.

"That's fantastic," I say, stroking the less devilish devil. "He seems to be doing well."

We talk more as he purrs, and when we're done, she tucks him into a cat carrier. "Thank you for that date last month. Even though it didn't go anywhere, it made me realize something."

"What's that?"

"That I needed to make a change. And I did."

"I'm glad it was helpful to you. And I'm glad it was helpful to Saul."

"The funny thing is, after I started seeing you about the cat, I met this guy online, and he's great. I went to dinner without taking Saul. Then to a movie."

"That's terrific progress."

She hoists the carrier onto her shoulder. "If things hadn't gone wrong with you, I never would've met this new guy." She pats the bag. "It's funny how things work out, isn't it?"

"Yeah. It is funny," I say with a small smile.

After the appointment, I take a lunch break, needing some exercise, so I ride to the town square in Duck Falls, and lock up my bike. But the way things work out feels less funny and more frustrating and annoying. It feels like things should work out in an entirely different way.

I still don't know what way that is, but it shouldn't be this.

I wander the town square, marinating on where I am in life. Where I want to be.

I pass the boba tea shop, and Nina waves to me. I stroll by the wine bar, and Oscar says hi as he sets up for the afternoon. I venture by the hair salon, where January's friend gives me a nod.

Do I miss New York?

Yes, but no.

All these people, all these places feel right to me.

That ought to be enough.

At the corner, I spot the hardware store, a reminder

that I need to snag a new light bulb to replace one that burned out. Best to focus on practical matters, not the ruminations of a half-empty heart.

I head inside and say hello to the two men who run the shop, Travis's dads. David points me to the light bulb section. I grab one, head to the counter, and say, "This is all I need today."

"Are you sure you know how to install it? Do you need help with that, vet?" David teases.

"I think I can figure it out. Connects to the dewclaw, right?"

"Sure, but if you can't get it sorted, you just be sure to ask the carpenter next door," David says, a little flirty, like he enjoys being in on the news about January and me.

Even though there is no January and me. Not like there was that day we ran into them.

I keep my grin fixed on my lips. "Sure. Will do, mate."

He rings me up, hands me the light bulb, and says, "We're having a barbecue next weekend. If you'd like to join us, it would be fun. The boys can play baseball."

"I'd love that." I leave, content that I'm making friends in this new town, right along with my son. That ought to be a good thing.

Plus, we're going to the dog shelter this weekend.

That'll be a great thing.

And even though my dad is facing plenty of challenges, he's holding up.

I see him often. Mum too.

All good things.

My clients are great. My practice is thriving. My son is happy.

The glass should be all the way full.

But it feels all the way empty.

I wander through the square some more, looking at my phone briefly when I see a text from Aunt Jane, thanking me for my latest pic of Ethan splashing in the pool.

Aunt Jane: Miss you, love. But life in California seems to be treating you well.

I'm not entirely sure what to say, so I reply with a smiley face. Then I delete the emoticon because I am not a smiley-face guy.

Instead, I type another answer.

Liam: Miss you too.

That feels true at the moment. I click to my next text.

Oliver: Did you ever figure out your fox issues?

This conversation requires a phone call. I ring him on FaceTime. He's in his Manhattan office, wearing a suit, and I'm in my scrubs. He looks me up and down. "I see we're both in our work uniforms."

"Seems we are." My tone is sullen, and I hate it. But I can't change it.

"You also look ridiculously sad. Are you still being a complete twat about relationships?"

I scrub a hand across the back of my neck, looking around. "I think I might be."

He laughs. "Yeah, you probably are. Didn't you break up with a woman you're in love with?"

"I sort of did."

"Judging from the look on your face, that was sort of dumb."

"Or maybe all the way dumb."

"So why'd you do it, then?"

"We don't want the same things." But even as I say it, that urge to expand my family, to add a baby to the mix, doesn't feel as important as it did when I met her. Not when faced with the thought of losing her.

He arches a brow. "Are you absolutely certain about that?"

Am I certain? I thought I was sure, but I don't know anymore.

When I don't say anything, Oliver fills the silence.

"It seems when you find somebody you love, really love, especially when you've never been in love before, you ought to try and make it work, Liam."

There's some serious wisdom in there, but I'm not actually sure how to mine it.

I hop on my bike and go back to work, because that I can do.

27

JANUARY

When I finish my job the next day installing kitchen cabinets for LaTanya Smith, Wednesday and I head to town, both of us on a mission.

Boba tea and YouTube channel planning for her and Audrey.

Advice and sympathy from Alva for me.

As we near the salon, Wednesday taps her wrist. "Did you know it's time?"

"Time for what? Seeing Audrey? Um, yeah. Obviously."

She pats my shoulder. "Ripley, Mom. Ripley. Keep up with me."

"This weekend," I say, doing my best to stay cheery for my girl.

When she spots Audrey snapping photos of some ducks in a pink wading pool, she waves and rushes off to hang with her bestie.

I go to see Alva at the salon.

She's closing up, and I sit in one of the chairs, look at her in the mirror, and sigh heavily.

I'm a sandbag made of lead.

My heart is stone.

My head hurts.

"Talk to me, babe."

The saddest sigh in the state of California falls from my lips. "I held this sweet little girl the other day, Betty's granddaughter, and it made me think maybe I could do this. I just don't want to lose him."

She stares at me in the mirror, an intensity in her brown eyes as she tucks her sleek black hair behind her ears. "You shouldn't have children for another person."

"I know that, but I like kids. Hell, I love kids." I don't sound as chipper as I want to.

"No doubt there. But just because you have one, just because you love them, doesn't mean you should have another one for a man. It's not fair to the kid, or to the man, or to you."

My chest aches, a nagging, insistent pain. "But I love him too, and I don't know what to do."

"If you don't know if you want children, you can't make yourself want them for him."

"I want to want them. I think maybe I could. When I held Betty's granddaughter, I thought maybe I could do it."

She turns around, facing me so we're no longer looking in the mirror. Somehow, stripping away that reflection makes the conversation more intense. She parks her hands on the armrests of the salon chair. "But you don't know for sure, right?"

My throat hitches. "I don't think I know for sure. But I don't want to lose him. I love him. I love him so much. More than I thought I would. So much that I'd marry him if he wanted," I say, and she lights up with glee. "So maybe I *should* be willing to have kids."

The glee winks off, replaced by a stern stare. "Have you told him any of this? How you feel about kids? About him? About a future? Not even the marrying part, but the being-willing-to-be-a-partner part? The *I love you and want to be with you always* part. Have you spoken to him about how you feel?"

I flash back through our conversations, because I have a sinking feeling I've said the opposite to Liam.

That day at IKEA, he asked if I wanted to settle down. I said I was still working up the nerve to adopt a cat.

He asked if my life was Wednesday and me against the world.

I said yes, and I liked it that way. *I can focus on my business, on my kid. I don't have to worry about a man.*

On the porch swing, he asked what were the chances of meeting someone who wants the same things you do.

I said small, and we toasted to the limited odds of it happening.

But we never really acknowledged that it could be us, that we *could* want the same thing at the same time.

I don't know if he wants what I want, but I know this—I haven't told him that nearly everything I said to him that day at IKEA has changed.

I no longer want to be me against the world.

I no longer want to *never* settle down.

I no longer want to avoid love.

And I haven't told him, either, that this—*us*—does feel like the right place at the right time, and with the right person too.

Maybe I've been seeing everything the wrong way.

Maybe wanting the same things isn't about more kids.

Maybe it's about commitment. About being a family.

In a burst of clarity, I wonder if I've been wrong about what he wants all along.

If I've been guessing.

And if maybe what he wants is precisely the thing that I can give him.

A promise that I could be his person.

28

LIAM

Ethan wakes me up early on Saturday, like it's Christmas morning.

He tugs my shirt. "Can we go now?"

Yawning, I flip onto my side. "Give a man a Saturday morning lie-in, would you?"

"You're zero fun."

"That is true."

But a cup of English breakfast, a shower, and a shave later, we're at the animal shelter.

He's bouncing, brimming with more energy than I've ever seen in him. He checks out nearly every dog. A beagle named Roxy, a golden retriever mix named Gecko, and some kind of white fluffy mutt named Button.

At the end of the next row of kennels, he stops cold, and in a hushed whisper, he says, "Look!"

I follow his gesture to see a min pin dachshund at the back of a cage, cowering in the corner, shaking.

Ethan runs to her. I follow. He beckons me to come

even closer, pointing at the brown-and-tan dog with the bat ears and big eyes. "Oh, Dad, look at her. She's so cute and so scared."

"She's absolutely adorable."

He stares at her a little longer, then turns to me. "Can we get her?"

I blink, surprised. "She doesn't seem like the type of dog you'd want. She's not a border collie mix or a shepherd mix like Katrina. I thought that was what you wanted?"

He shakes his head adamantly, pointing to the pooch in the corner, all ten pounds of her by the looks of it. "I want that dog," he says, and it's the most earnest, honest thing anyone has ever said in the history of the world.

He sweeps his gaze back to me, his eyes big and blue and vulnerable. "She's just sitting in the corner, and she's shaking, and she looks sad. Just look at her."

She does look sad. She also looks like she needs a home. I take a look at the index card describing her. She's two and a half.

The woman who runs the rescue walks by, dreadlocks in her hair. She stops and flashes us a warm smile, tossing her hair back over her shoulder. "I see you've met Ruby. She's a sweetheart. She's an owner surrender. Just came in the other day."

Owner surrenders can mean a number of things, from someone who was evicted to someone who didn't want the dog anymore, from sickness to behavior problems. "Is there any particular reason she was a surrender?"

The woman's expression shifts into a sad smile. "The

man who had her went into hospice, so we took his dog."

My heart winces like someone has just tightened it with a rope, knotting it into the smallest shape possible.

"Dad. Can we give her a home?"

I look at the dog again—this sweet, sad animal who no longer has a person, who probably wants a person more than anything, who wants love and a home.

Isn't that all anyone wants?

That's what I've given my son.

That's why he's thrived, why he's happy.

And why I am too.

Just like that, the glass fills up.

There is no longer a rope around my heart. Everything in it makes sense.

My eyes well with a sheen of tears. One slides down my cheek. Ethan must notice because he grabs my hand, squeezes it, and sets his head against my side. I wipe away the rebel tear.

The woman says in a soft voice, "He was very good to her. He loved her very much."

That doesn't do anything to help with the leaking eyeballs. I try to hold back the onslaught of emotions as I think about my son's mother and how much she must have loved Ethan for him to come to me so full of love already.

Instead of tightening, my heart grows bigger. It swells like it needs more room, like it needs to run across the room, fling open the window, and let in more sunlight.

Ethan pleads one more time. "Can we get her, please? She needs us."

One more peek at the sweet, scared little min pin dachshund, and I am certain his words are the only ones that matter. "She does need us."

The woman steps into the kennel, picks up the nervous dog, and carries her to us as we sit on a bench.

She hands the dog to Ethan. He wraps his arms around her. Ruby's still trembling, but she gazes up at him like she's found her home.

She licks his face . . .

And a boy falls in love with a dog.

He laughs and nuzzles her, then whispers in her big, floppy ear, "I think you were happy before. I think you had steak and played with Frisbees, and you went for swims and you took long walks and you panted when it was hot out and you smiled when you were happy and you slept under the covers."

Yes, the windows are open.

The doors too.

Because now I know what January was trying to tell me.

What I wanted to believe but didn't quite know how.

You can write your own narrative. You can tell your own story.

I squeeze his shoulder, emotions flooding me, clogging my throat. "She sounds a lot like you before we met."

"That's why she's our dog. Right?"

I haul him and Ruby in for a huge hug, boy and dog. "She's our dog, and you're my son."

* * *

We go home with Ruby, and along the way, Ethan changes her name to Steve Trout.

It's the worst possible name for so many reasons, but I don't care. Once we're home, we go through the garage so he can hunt for a Frisbee.

"I'm going to teach her how to catch it," he says.

"I can't wait to see her new skills."

But when I pop onto the front porch to check the mail, I'm a bit distracted. I find a Pyrex dish by the door.

It's full of pink cupcakes. There's a note on top. With eager fingers and a wildly beating heart, I reach for the note then unfold it.

I am a forensic scientist. I am a crime scene investigator. And this handwriting is the only one I want to see.

It's the handwriting of the woman I want to be my person.

I made these for you, and I have something to tell you.
I. Love. You.
I want to talk to you, and I have things to say to you, and I want to say them before I lose you, because I don't want to lose you. And I will do just about anything to keep you.

I pop into the backyard and tell Ethan to keep an eye on Steve Trout, but he doesn't even need me to tell him, since he has yet to take his eyes off her.

With long, determined strides, I make my way across the yard, and I knock on January's door.

29

———

LIAM

She looks gorgeous.

No surprise.

She looks hopeful too, but nervous.

She looks like I feel.

"Hi," she says, sounding wobbly.

"I want to talk to you," I blurt out.

Words tumble from her. "Did you get the cupcakes? My note?"

"Yes, and I loved it. All of it," I say, and her lips relax into a gorgeous smile. "And I have so much to say too, starting with . . . I got a dog."

She clasps her hand to her mouth, excitement lighting up those gorgeous blue eyes. "Tell me all about the dog."

"That's the thing. I want to tell you about the dog. I want to tell you a million things, but I want to tell you something first. And it's this—I did it all wrong when I told you I was falling in love with you." I smack my forehead. "Who the hell says, 'I'm falling in love with you,' and then breaks it off?"

She laughs lightly.

"I'm a daft idiot," I say.

"No, you're not."

I reach for her hand, and she lets me take it. "I am in love with you. I love you. I want to be with you."

Her eyes go wide, and then tears start to fall from them. "I love you too, and I want that too, but, Liam, I have to tell you something."

"Tell me." But I know that whatever it is, it'll be fine.

Because I know what I want.

And it's her.

I'm pretty sure that's what she's offering.

Still, a gentleman should listen.

She takes a deep breath. "I know you want more kids, and I've thought about that a lot, and whether I want them. I want to tell you that if it's important to you, we can talk more about it, but I'm not sure my feelings about more children will change. But that's the *only* thing I'm not sure about. I'm thirty-seven years old, and I've never been in love, and then you came into my life, and I am wildly in love. I love you," she says.

And my heart does that thing again. It fills. It floods. It expands.

"I love you so much," I tell her. It feels so good to say that.

January isn't done though. "I'm so afraid that the way I feel won't be enough for you. But I'm going to tell you anyway. You're the one." She grabs my shirt like she needs to be close to me. And I want her close. "I don't want to be just a woman against the world. I want it to be you and me against the world—you, me, and Wednesday and Ethan. I don't know if that's what you want, and it's scary and crazy to put myself out there, but as I look back on the last month, I think I've given you the impression that I don't want any of that."

Her words come in a rush of emotions that I want to cup in my hand, to hold, to keep safe. "But now it's all I want. You're all I want. Is that enough for you? If we don't have more children? Is it enough if it's you and me and us, and the dog?"

I laugh, grab her, and wrap her in my arms. "Yes. That's what I want. And I'm stupid for not having realized it before. I'm incredibly foolish for missing it."

I pull back, and she looks up at me, her expression lovely and vulnerable. "Are you sure? How can you say that?"

I run a hand along her hair. "You are enough for me. You're so much more than enough for me. It took me adopting this dog to realize that I was looking at everything the wrong way. I thought I needed to have more children. I thought about how I missed seven years of my son's life, and if I had another kid, I wouldn't miss a moment. But then you said something to me." I pause for a breath as the memory rushes back—one that was never far from the surface. "You said to write our own narrative. And that didn't fully resonate until today when we got this dog, and I realized that writing her story was *all* we could do, and we did, and it's a great story. And everything became clear."

She grins, like she's wildly happy too. "What became clear?"

"What I wanted was *not* to have missed the first seven years of Ethan's life, but that can't change, and having another kid won't make up for it. But I don't need to make up for it. I have to let it go, and I did. All I want to do is live my life with him and with you and your daughter, and I want to write our story together."

"Me too," she says, her soft words hooking into my heart.

I take her hands, holding them tight. "That's all I want now. I want to love my son, and I want to love this amazing woman in front of me, and I want to love this dog we just adopted. I have so much love inside me, and I want to give it to all of you, and honestly, I'd love to give it to your daughter if she'll let me."

"You would? Really?" Her voice trembles like she can't believe I'm truly saying this.

But I am, and I mean every word.

"I am perfectly good with this. With the family we already have. All I want is not to miss a second of what comes our way. I don't want to miss a minute of what we will have together. Because I know we can have an amazing life. And I know we can have an amazing family. You and me and Ethan and Wednesday and Steve Trout and Ripley."

She arches a brow in a question. "Steve Trout?"

I wave my hand. "He named the dog Steve Trout. It's a girl. None of it makes any sense."

"It makes perfect sense. He named the dog after someone he likes."

"Like you're going to do with Ripley. When you're ready, say the word. You will have free vet care for life, even at-home service. I am a cat whisperer, you know. Saul is living proof of that."

She laughs. "That's a really good promise."

"See? That's what I want. I want to promise you things and deliver on them. I want to promise you my heart and give it to you. I don't want anything more than what I'm already hoping we can have together. Do you want that?"

And I wait for her answer, wildly hoping that it's going to match what I learned today.

She lifts her hands to my face. "I love you, Liam. I want to be with you. I want to be the person that you came here and found. And I think we could have a great family together with the family we already have. And I want to put my heart on the line for you. So yes, I want that."

I draw her against me, looking around at everything that we have, a wonderful embarrassment of riches. "This is all I could ever want."

I kiss her. On the scale of kisses, it's right there at the top. It's long and soft and slow. It's passionate and sensual and full of love.

When we break apart, she gasps.

The excited kind of gasp, not the sexy kind.

"What is it?"

"Wednesday wants to get a cat. Let's make it a double today. Want to go find Ripley?"

I grin, and it takes over my whole being. "The four of us?"

She rolls her eyes. "Obviously."

"Such cheek," I say, shaking my head.

She grabs my hand, slides it around to her ass, and whispers, "You love my cheeks."

Cracking up, I answer, "So very much."

Later that day, the five of us squeeze into her truck—Steve Trout on Ethan's lap, an inseparable pair already—return to the same shelter, and find an adorable black-and-white tuxedo cat.

January strokes the cat's chin and says, "You're Ripley."

I look at the cutie and say, "Looks more like a Five O'clock."

Ethan suggests Dolphin.

Wednesday shakes her head. "You're all wrong. She's The Hacker."

It's a perfect name. And I think I might have a life that's pretty damn close to perfect too.

30

JANUARY

What's better than realizing the guy next door is the love of your life?

What's better than him feeling the same way about you?

One thing. *One thing only.*

Sex with that guy that night.

I sneak over, because it's fun to sneak over.

After opening the door slowly and ever so quietly, he tugs me inside, then brings his finger to his lips.

Is Ethan awake? I mouth, surprised at the secrecy routine, since his kid is the king of sleeping like a log.

"Steve Trout does not sleep as soundly as Ethan."

"Ah," I whisper, nodding, and we both tiptoe across the living room to Liam's bedroom. He shuts the door and jerks me against him.

He's not soft and gentle.

He's ravenous and demanding. His hands rope into my hair, and he tugs hard on my strands, dropping his fantastic lips to my neck. Kissing me greedily. Kissing me like he's starving. In seconds, his lips are on my mouth, and he devours me.

I am liquid in his arms.

Bliss flows through me.

Desire surges over my skin, drowns my bones, my cells.

My hands travel up his chest, grabbing at him just as he grabs at me. And soon, we are two frenzied, fevered creatures.

Driven mad with longing.

With lust.

And now, with love.

He lifts me up, hooks my legs around his waist, and carries me to the bed. "It's been too long."

"I know. It was a miserable week. I climbed the walls," I whisper as I tear at his T-shirt, jerking it over his head.

"That should never happen again," he says, stripping me in seconds flat.

"Yes. Don't ever do that again," I say, shuddering as his hands roam down my naked body, gliding over my breasts, my belly, my thighs.

He steps back, undoes his jeans, then returns to me, parting my legs.

"You have my word. I will always be here to fuck you," he growls as he moves between my thighs, settling there, then notching the head of his cock against me.

I arch up, eager, hungry. My hand darts out, grabbing his length, guiding him home.

"So greedy."

"I know what I want," I say.

"You do, and I love that about you," he says, sliding into me, then groaning as he fills me.

Pleasure tears mercilessly across my entire body as Liam thrusts into me. His right hand slides down my leg, grips my knee, and pushes it up high against my chest.

"Yes," I moan, grabbing his ass, holding on tight. "I love this," I whisper, words falling from my lips, sensations spreading wildly through every molecule. But those words don't feel like enough. And even though I never thought I'd be one of those heat-of-the-moment people, I also never thought I'd feel so much for one person, and I need to say what's in my heart.

I lift my hands, hold his stubbled face, and meet his gaze.

He slows down. "You okay, love?"

There it is again.

Love.

"I love this. I love *you*," I say, and it comes out needy, breathy, and full of passion.

"Love you so much," he answers.

And that's all. That's all I needed to say. But saying it makes the most amazing sex somehow even better.

Because it's fucking, and it's making love, and it's forever.

It's all of those things I didn't think I wanted.

And it's everything I love having.

When we come together, lost in each other, we pant, moan, and collapse.

I murmur, lazily stroking his back, "You're kind of a sex machine."

"And this is a problem?"

I laugh, shaking my head. "I like machines."

He eases out of me. "Good. Because this machine is always ready to do the job," he says, then heads to the bathroom and returns seconds later with a warm, wet washcloth to clean me up.

After he tosses it in the hamper, he returns to my side, drawing me close. "Was that makeup sex?"

"Kind of," I whisper.

"Should we break up again to have it?"

I swat his chest. "Take that back."

He laughs, then presses a soft kiss to my shoulder as something scratches at the door.

Or rather, someone.

With four legs.

He rises and opens the door slightly. Steve Trout bounds in, leaps onto the bed, and sniffs my shoulder. I'm glad that's where her snout goes.

I laugh. "Your dog likes the way I smell."

"The dog has excellent taste."

Liam returns to the bed again, looping an arm around me and the dog too, who is tucking herself into my armpit. "You should sometime, you know, spend the night," he says.

"I know. I should. Maybe when Wednesday goes to Audrey's house for a sleepover. I don't mind slipping out for an hour or so when she's home, but I can't stay long."

He sighs heavily. "If only there was a way to solve that problem."

I shoot him a curious look. "Like build an underground tunnel between our homes?"

"That or move in together," he says, flashing me a *you know you want to* grin.

"But I have a house," I say, though, even as I say it, I do love the idea of being with him every day and night. After all, that's what we both said we wanted.

"Yeah, so do I," he says, tapping his chin. "Hmm. I like mine. And you like yours. Fine, we'll build a concourse between them, like two terminals at the airport."

I laugh. "Are you really asking me to move in?"

"Woman, I told you I want to spend the rest of my life with you. Yeah, soon I'd like it not to be in separate homes."

The thought should scare me.

But it doesn't.

Not at all.

Not in the least.

I want all of that with him, with all of us.

I tap his nose. "Why don't we look for a place that's ours, then?"

"That sounds like a brilliant plan from a brilliant woman"—he takes a beat—"who wants to get in my trousers every night."

I roll my eyes. "Duh. You *are* good in bed."

"As advertised."

"And in the kitchen."

"Admit it, I'm a catch."

I kiss him again. "You're a man-i-corn."

"That sounds dirty and sweet at the same time."

"Just like you."

He gives me yet another kiss. "And just like you too, love."

Love.

Yes, that's what he calls me in and out of bed, and I love it all the time. Because it turns out he's the right person in the right place and at the right time.

31

———

LIAM

The next few months fly by in a blur.

I treat patients, spay cats and dogs, administer shots, and tend to both broken and full hearts at my practice. All in a day's work as a vet.

I visit my dad a lot. He's making the best of things, with laughter and jokes and lots of long conversations.

Not only with me, but with Ethan, though Ethan is often distracted by the need to ringmaster his three-dog circus, taking Steve Trout into the backyard with the musical girls, tossing Frisbees to all of them, and inviting lots of face licks.

So the conversations fall to Mum and me, or January and me, or to Wednesday.

Funny thing I didn't see coming—Wednesday gets on great with my dad. She reads articles to him on new trends in website design, then blog posts on ethical hacking trends, and she likes to describe the sites she's working on to him. It helps her design, she says, to have to give them words so he can visualize them.

And he likes hearing about it.

And likes weighing in too, offering her tips now and then.

Some of them she takes.

Mum paid January to fix the cupboards.

She was determined to win that battle, but January won too, giving the money immediately to a reading-for-the-blind charity.

We do other things together, like go to parents' nights at both the elementary school and high school, and to dinner at the sandwich shop we all like, and to the bowling alley.

January beats us all at bowling.

She's good with her hands.

And those skills intrigue Ethan, it turns out. He asks her to help him build a doghouse for Steve Trout, so one day in November, they go to the hardware store run by his friend's dads and pick up the wood and other supplies, then she spends the day teaching him how to build.

Honestly, it's the best thing I've ever seen. *In my entire life.* Especially since Steve seems to dig the doghouse.

For about a minute.

Which makes us all laugh.

The next day, Wednesday asks me to teach The Hacker a trick.

"Cats aren't very good at tricks," I say.

"I know that. But how about a high five? I have a potential client who makes cat toys, and I want to send a video to impress her to win the deal."

"By all means, then, let's do it."

A few days and several thousand pieces of tuna later, and The Hacker can work a high paw like no one's business.

* * *

By the time the holidays roll around, the woman I love begins work on a new expansion project.

Not *that*.

She hires some additional contractors and begins expanding the attic in my home.

In the end, we decided we liked this house.

The pool helps a lot.

But teenage girls need more space, so January devised the brilliant idea to make this home bigger, and then rent hers next door. As for that accent wall she wanted, she painted one wall in the living room pink.

My bachelor-pad vibe has been crushed, julienned, and chopped to pieces, and I couldn't be happier.

One fine day in December, as she's finishing up work in the attic, I pop upstairs, enjoying the sight of her in her work clothes. What can I say? January and her hammer have always done it for me.

I rap on the doorframe.

She must see me out of the corner of her eye, because she hits pause on her phone and removes an AirPod.

"Are you trying to finagle a quickie?"

"Is a quickie an option? Because sure."

She laughs. "It's usually an option."

"I'll take it, then, but mostly I wanted to know if you wanted to go for a drive when you're done?"

"A drive?" she asks suspiciously.

"Yeah, that thing you do in cars and trucks?"

She rolls her eyes. "Sure. But don't think I don't know that you're trying to take me to some lovers' lane and park."

I shrug sheepishly. "Maybe I am."

* * *

Later, after she showers, we hop in the truck and go for a drive. Something we used to do when we were first dating.

Something we've kept up.

It's fun sneaking off.

Especially in a small town full of rolling hills, wineries, and train tracks that occasionally glitter.

Seems fitting.

I point to a side road that runs along the tracks. "Let's go there."

"As you wish," she says, and soon we pull over, get out, and walk along the tracks while the sun dips in the sky.

The days are shorter now, but this being California, the weather is still warm enough for a walk without jackets.

As we wander, we talk about our plans for the holidays, seeing friends and family, being together, and all that good stuff.

The plans are nothing out of the ordinary.

It's just us, doing life, living it every second.

Which makes it all the more fitting that this moment is the one where I stop, tug her close, and drop to one knee. I waste no time. I cut to the chase. I ask the question we've both known was coming. "Will you marry me?"

She laughs, then she sinks down to the ground. "I thought you'd never ask."

"Hey, it's not like I waited that long," I say, cupping her cheeks.

"Three months. Such an eternity."

"You knew it was coming."

"I did, but I'm still happy, Liam."

"Me too."

I reach into my pocket, take out a box, and show her the ring that Alva and Wednesday helped me pick out last month. The joking ceases when January sees it. The diamonds catch the light from the fading sun. They're all laid out in a platinum band, ideal for a carpenter.

"Oh my God. It's perfect for me," she says, a smile lighting up her whole face as she gazes at the ring.

Pride suffuses me, along with love, certainty, and so much happiness. "I wanted it to be one you could wear while working. I want it to be one that makes you happy, that feels like yours."

She swallows, twin tears slipping down her cheeks as she holds my face. "You feel like mine. And I love you."

"And I love you, but let's put that ring on."

She lets go, waves a hand in front of her face like she

needs to settle her tears, then exhales. I slide the ring onto her finger, and we admire the diamonds.

When she lifts her head, she whispers, "What are the chances you meet the right person at the right time in the right place?"

"If he moves next door to you, I'd say they're pretty damn good."

She grins, gazes at the ring once more, then says, "I'll take those chances every day for the rest of my life."

"Good, because I want to spend the rest of my life with you."

And we kiss as the sun sets over this small town that's become my new home, where all the glasses are full.

EPILOGUE

Liam

By the next summer, The Hacker can sit on command, roll over, play dead, and go for walks, all thanks to Wednesday.

"I hacked all the dog training tips I could find and engineered them for cats," she says one Saturday morning as we take the pets for a stroll.

"Steve can do all those things too, and she can sit up and beg, and shake, so I'm kind of winning," I point out.

"That only makes me want to teach The Hacker to retrieve radishes and bring them to your bed," she counters.

January laughs, giving me *she got you* eyes.

Ethan laughs. "Do it, please. That would slap so hard."

"I'd pay good money to wake up with broccoli or

radishes next to my fiancé," January says, reaching for my hand.

"Not fiancé for much longer," I add.

In fact, a few hours later, in the town square with my mum and dad, my sisters, their kids, January's family, and all our friends looking on, including Oliver, Summer, and Aunt Jane from New York, plus Alva, Audrey, Missy, and Betty, the woman I moved next door to walks down the grass, joins me in the gazebo, and hands the bouquet of daisies to her daughter.

When the justice of the peace asks if I promise to love, honor, and cherish January for the rest of my life, I say yes, and my heart soars when she says the same.

"And now the rings," the justice of the peace says.

My son hands them to me. I slide a band on January's finger, matching her diamond band, and she slides one on me.

Then I kiss the bride as the ducks wade in the pink pools and glitter sparkles on the pavement, and I am happy with all the family I have.

Living every moment.

And loving every second of it.

* * *

Eager for more sexy rom coms? Be sure to try my brand new standalone romance, My So-Called Sex-Life! It's FREE IN KU!

Binge the entire Guys Who Got Away series FREE in KU!

Birthday Suit: Leo & Lulu/Friends to Lovers/Best
Friend's Ex
Dear Sexy Ex-Boyfriend: Oliver & Summer/Friends to
Lovers/Fake Fiancée
The What If Guy: Logan & Bryn/Boss/Employee
Thanks for Last Night: Ransom & Teagan/Friends to
Lovers/Player Auction
The Dream Guy Next Door: Liam and
January/Neighbors to Lovers/Single Parents
Lucky Suit: Kristen and Cameron/Mistaken Identity
And
A Guy Walks Into My Bar, an MM standalone spinoff:
Dean and Fitz

BE A LOVELY

Want to be the first to know of sales, new releases, special deals and giveaways? Sign up for my newsletter today!

Want to be part of a fun, feel-good place to talk about books and romance, and get sneak peeks of covers and advance copies of my books? Be a Lovely!

MORE BOOKS BY LAUREN

I've written more than 100 books! **All of these titles below
are FREE in Kindle Unlimited!**

Double Pucked

A sexy, outrageous MFM hockey romantic comedy!

Puck Yes

A fake marriage, spicy MFM hockey rom com!

The Virgin Society Series

Meet the Virgin Society – great friends who'd do anything for
each other. Indulge in these forbidden, emotionally-charged,
and wildly sexy age-gap romances!

The RSVP

The Tryst

The Tease

The Dating Games Series

A fun, sexy romantic comedy series about friends in the city
and their dating mishaps!

The Virgin Next Door

Two A Day

The Good Guy Challenge

How To Date Series (New and ongoing)

Four great friends. Four chances to learn how to date

again. Four standalone romantic comedies full of love, sex and meet-cute shenanigans.

My So-Called Sex Life

Plays Well With Others

A romantic comedy adventure standalone

A Real Good Bad Thing

Boyfriend Material

Four fabulous heroines. Four outrageous proposals. Four chances at love in this sexy rom-com series!

Asking For a Friend

Sex and Other Shiny Objects

One Night Stand-In

Overnight Service

Big Rock Series

My #1 New York Times Bestselling sexy as sin, irreverent, male-POV romantic comedy!

Big Rock

Mister O

Well Hung

Full Package

Joy Ride

Hard Wood

Happy Endings Series

Romance starts with a bang in this series of standalones following a group of friends seeking and avoiding love!

Come Again

Shut Up and Kiss Me

Kismet

My Single-Versary

Ballers And Babes

Sexy sports romance standalones guaranteed to make you hot!

Most Valuable Playboy

Most Likely to Score

A Wild Card Kiss

Rules of Love Series

Athlete, virgins and weddings!

The Virgin Rule Book

The Virgin Game Plan

The Virgin Replay

The Virgin Scorecard

The Extravagant Series

Bodyguards, billionaires and hoteliers in this sexy, high-stakes series of standalones!

One Night Only

One Exquisite Touch

My One-Week Husband

The Guys Who Got Away Series

Friends in New York City and California fall in love in this fun and hot rom-com series!

Birthday Suit

Dear Sexy Ex-Boyfriend

The What If Guy

Thanks for Last Night

The Dream Guy Next Door

Always Satisfied Series

A group of friends in New York City find love and laughter in this series of sexy standalones!

Satisfaction Guaranteed

Never Have I Ever

Instant Gratification

PS It's Always Been You

The Gift Series

An after dark series of standalones! Explore your fantasies!

The Engagement Gift

The Virgin Gift

The Decadent Gift

The Heartbreakers Series

Three brothers. Three rockers. Three standalone sexy romantic comedies.

Once Upon a Real Good Time

Once Upon a Sure Thing

Once Upon a Wild Fling

Sinful Men

A high-stakes, high-octane, sexy-as-sin romantic suspense series!

My Sinful Nights

My Sinful Desire

My Sinful Longing

My Sinful Love

My Sinful Temptation

From Paris With Love

Swoony, sweeping romances set in Paris!

Wanderlust

Part-Time Lover

One Love Series

A group of friends in New York falls in love one by one in this sexy rom-com series!

The Sexy One

The Hot One

The Knocked Up Plan

Come As You Are

Lucky In Love Series

A small town romance full of heat and blue collar heroes and sexy heroines!

Best Laid Plans

The Feel Good Factor

Nobody Does It Better

Unzipped

No Regrets

An angsty, sexy, emotional, new adult trilogy about one young couple fighting to break free of their pasts!

The Start of Us

The Thrill of It

Every Second With You

The Caught Up in Love Series

A group of friends finds love!

The Pretending Plot

The Dating Proposal

The Second Chance Plan

The Private Rehearsal

Seductive Nights Series

A high heat series full of danger and spice!

Night After Night

After This Night

One More Night

A Wildly Seductive Night

Joy Delivered Duet

A high-heat, wickedly sexy series of standalones that will set
your sheets on fire!

Nights With Him

Forbidden Nights

Unbreak My Heart

A standalone second chance emotional roller coaster of a
romance

The Muse

A magical realism romance set in Paris

Good Love Series of sexy rom-coms co-written with Lili Valente!

I also write MM romance under the name L. Blakely!

Hopelessly Bromantic Duet (MM)

Roomies to lovers to enemies to fake boyfriends

Hopelessly Bromantic

Here Comes My Man

Men of Summer Series (MM)

Two baseball players on the same team fall in love in a forbidden romance spanning five epic years

Scoring With Him

Winning With Him

All In With Him

MM Standalone Novels

A Guy Walks Into My Bar

The Bromance Zone

One Time Only

The Best Men (Co-written with Sarina Bowen)

Winner Takes All Series (MM)

A series of emotionally-charged and irresistibly sexy standalone MM sports romances!

The Boyfriend Comeback

Turn Me On

A Very Filthy Game

Limited Edition Husband

Manhandled

If you want a personalized recommendation, email me at
laurenblakelybooks@gmail.com!

CONTACT

I love hearing from readers! You can find me on TikTok at LaurenBlakelyBooks, Instagram at LaurenBlakely-Books, Facebook at LaurenBlakelyBooks, or online at LaurenBlakely.com. You can also email me at lauren blakelybooks@gmail.com